He was proposing a kind of sexual blackmail

"You belong to me, Sian. I won't let you throw yourself away on another man."

"You can't stop me," she said.

"No?" Jarrett murmured. "And if I refuse to stop seeing Bethany until you come to me?"

Her eyes widened in disbelief. "You wouldn't," she whispered.

"I would," he said curtly. "And Bethany is far from averse to my making love to her."

"Jarrett—"

"My life depends on this, Sian. Until you come to me I shall continue to see Bethany. It would be a pity to seduce your sister in an effort to bring you to your senses."

"That would only make me hate you more!"

"I'd rather have your hate than nothing," he said. "And make up your mind soon, Sian. Because otherwise I won't be responsible for the consequences."

Harlequin Presents
by Carole Mortimer

These books may be available at your local bookseller.

For a free catalog listing all titles currently available, send your name and address to:

Harlequin Reader Service
P.O. Box 52040, Phoenix, AZ 85072-9988
Canadian address: Stratford, Ontario N5A 6W2

CAROLE MORTIMER

trust in summer madness

Harlequin Books

TORONTO • NEW YORK • LONDON
AMSTERDAM • PARIS • SYDNEY • HAMBURG
STOCKHOLM • ATHENS • TOKYO • MILAN

For
John and Matthew

———————◆·◆·◆———————

Harlequin Presents first edition February 1984
ISBN 0-373-10669-6

Original hardcover edition published in 1983
by Mills & Boon Limited

CHAPTER ONE

'HEY, Sian, have you heard the news—Jarrett King is coming back!' Ginny cried excitedly as she bounded back into the office, her short dark hair framing her gaminely attractive face, her eyes a deep smoky blue, her lashes long and dark.

Jarrett King is coming back . . . Sian had waited three years to hear those words, and now it was too late!

Her hands shook as she continued to file the cards away under the name of the animal's owner, morning surgery in this busy veterinary surgery over half an hour ago; the daily ritual of putting the cards back in the files was part of her job as receptionist and secretary.

'Sian, did you hear what I said?' Ginny had just come back from an early lunch, an afternoon of operations as her brother, Chris Newman's, assistant ahead of her. 'I said—'

'I heard you.' Sian stood up to put the drawer back in its slot before going on to take out the next drawer. 'Someone has been in these files again,' she muttered, taking a P card out of the R section and refiling it.

'Probably Chris,' his sister dismissed, sitting on the edge of Sian's desk in the reception area. 'He's hopelessly untidy. Mum's in despair of him at home.'

Sian knew all about Chris's untidiness, and of Sara's constant complaining about it, and she preferred to think of it as forgetfulness. Chris was a dedicated vet, often preoccupied, and hopeless when it came to the paperwork involved. Luckily Sian had been able to take away most of the pressure of that since coming to work for him two years ago.

Ginny looked put out. 'Aren't you in the least interested in the fact that Jarrett King is coming to Swannell?'

Again that slight trembling of her hand at the mention of his name, even after all this time. 'Should I be?' Sian asked coolly, marvelling at the way she could remain so composed.

But with her flaming red hair and fiery hazel eyes she was the level-headed one of her family, the one who thought with logic and not emotions, and she knew that just because Jarrett was coming back here it didn't follow that she would see him. The opposite, she would have thought!

Sian moved about the office with all the grace of a young gazelle, her legs long and shapely, her body curved in all the right places for her gender, but slenderly so, the brown tailored skirt and fitted cream blouse giving her a look of cool efficiency.

'I would have thought so,' Ginny continued stubbornly.

Sian's dark brown brows rose, her lashes the same naturally dark colour. 'I don't understand your interest in the man, Ginny,' she mocked gently. 'He'd moved from Swannell before you even came to live here.'

'Everyone knows *of* Jarrett King,' the other girl scorned; she was a girl of Sian's own age, twenty-two, and had been happily married to the other vet in the practice, Martin Scott, for the last eighteen months.

And Ginny was right, everyone did know of Jarrett King. At least, in Swannell they did. He was the local man made good, the one who had left this small town to control a multi-million-pound building empire in America, taking over from his uncle. For years Jarrett had run the English side of the business, but he had soon put his own personalised stamp on the whole of the King building empire. Yes, everyone knew Jarrett King in Swannell, despite the fact that he had only lived here for five years before leaving, and none better than her.

'And I heard that you more than knew him once,' Ginny added slyly.

Sian's breathing seemed to stop—and then start again. 'Really?' she enquired coolly. 'I won't ask which gossip told you that.'

'And I won't tell you! Oh, Sian, I didn't mean to be bitchy,' Ginny was genuinely contrite, the two of them had a good friendship, 'but I thought you would show more interest than this.'

Sian smiled. 'I'm sorry to disappoint you, love, but Jarrett King's comings and goings to Swannell don't interest me in the least.'

'He hasn't been here for three years—you make it sound as if he flits back and forth from America all the time!'

Sian shrugged. 'I doubt he'll stay long this time.'

'I heard—'

'Ginny, for God's sake get in here!' Chris stood agitatedly in the doorway to the surgery. 'I've been waiting for you for over ten minutes. I'd like to get started—if you wouldn't mind?' he finished with biting sarcasm.

'I don't mind at all, brother dear,' Ginny smiled sweetly.

'Well?' he prompted impatiently as she made no effort to join him.

Ginny looked unimpressed with his anger. 'I'll be with you in a moment.'

He closed the door, muttering something about the unreliability of working with one's family.

Ginny grinned. 'He knows I'm a damned good assistant.'

'Modest too,' teased Sian, relieved to have the pressure off her.

Ginny slid off the desk-top. 'I suppose I'd better go and help him, he might do the unexpected and get nasty if he's kept waiting any longer.'

'That didn't seem to bother you a few seconds ago,' Sian laughed, feeling on safer ground now that they were no longer talking about Jarrett.

Ginny grimaced. 'I lived with him for twenty years, and he doesn't frighten me. He could have paid you a bit more attention, though. You are engaged.'

'We're also at work,' Sian reminded her dryly.

'So what, Martin often sneaks me a kiss.' Ginny walked to the door. 'But not Chris. I don't know what you see in him.' She frowned.

Sian laughed. 'That's because you're his sister.'

'Maybe,' Ginny smiled, going through to the surgery.

As soon as she could Sian tidied up her desk and left for the afternoon, locking the door behind her. The afternoon was hers until four, when she came back for the evening surgery.

At least, it should have been. But she had the shopping for lunch to do, had to get home in time to cook the meal for her father and sister. They always had a hot meal at lunchtime; her own job at the surgery and her sister's job as a hairdresser meant it wasn't practical to cook in the evenings, and they just grabbed a snack when they got in.

But today she didn't shop with her usual speed, finding herself thinking of Jarrett in spite of herself.

Could he really be coming back to Swannell? Could he *already* be back? After three years it didn't seem very likely, but even so she was wary as she walked around the shops, thinking she was going to walk into him around every street corner.

Swannell was a small rural town, and Sian's family were known to most people; she acknowledged several people as she bought the meat for lunch. She received curious looks in return to her open smile, and it began to dawn on her that Ginny could actually be right about Jarrett's return. Most people in this town knew of her association with Jarrett in the past, and they would be curious as to her reaction to his return now. Thank goodness she had been pre-warned by Ginny!

Her smile was bright and assured as she made her way to the Victorian-style house that was the home of her father, her sister and herself, her mother having died several years ago. The yellow Mini in the driveway told her that Bethany was already at home.

There was no sign of her sister in the kitchen, but the radio could be heard playing upstairs. Sian began to unpack her shopping, putting on the grill to cook the steak. Bethany would soon come down when she smelt the food cooking.

Sian's movements were automatic, her thoughts disturbed. If Jarrett really were coming back, and it looked as if he was, then it was inevitable that they should meet at some time; the town was hardly big enough for them to ignore each other. How was she going to stand that? She was the calm, practical one, and yet about Jarrett she had certainly never been either of those things.

But she was an engaged lady now, with a solitaire diamond ring on her left hand that said her heart and loyalty belonged to Chris. The mad, impetuous feelings she had once felt for Jarrett were a thing of the past, belonged to her childhood. As he would find out if he ever tried to remind her of them.

But she had no reason to suppose Jarrett would even remember her; she was probably one of the women he would rather forget, her stubbornness where he was concerned meaning that for once Jarrett hadn't had things completely his own way. And three years was a long time, a very long time.

'Hi,' her sister came into the kitchen, throwing her apple-core into the bin. 'I couldn't wait,' she grimaced at Sian's disapproving look, and sat down at the kitchen table, wearing denims and a loose blouse, her usual attire for working in the hairdressing salon. With her baby-blonde curls and placid blue eyes Bethany was the fiery one of the family; their father often teased them about their mixed-up natures.

'Lay the table,' Sian instructed her sister, wondering how Bethany ever managed to keep her slender figure with the amount of food she ate.

With a shrug Bethany did as requested. 'Hey, guess what I heard today?' Her expression suddenly brightened. 'Guess who's coming back to town?'

'Jarrett King,' Sian answered easily, more than ever glad Ginny had pre-warned her. Bethany had known all about Jarrett and herself in the past, and she felt relieved to be able to remain unruffled in front of her sister.

Bethany frowned her disappointment. 'How did you know?'

'News travels fast in a place this size,' Sian shrugged.

'And I thought I had a hot piece of gossip!'

'Don't worry,' she smiled. 'You probably have. Ginny just got in first.'

'She always does,' Bethany said without rancour.

'Still,' her expression brightened again, 'isn't it exciting about Jarrett coming back?'

Exciting? That was the last thing Sian would have called it! Three years, *three years* he had been away, and he had to come back *now*. Not next year or the year after that, when it wouldn't have mattered, but now.

'As I remember it, you never liked him,' she reminded her young sister.

Bethany flushed. 'I was a child three years ago, only sixteen—'

'You thought you were very grown up!'

'Well, I wasn't,' she snapped. 'Otherwise I would have known what a good-looking man Jarrett is.'

'You've seen him!' Sian's voice was sharp, although as she was turned towards the cooker Bethany couldn't possibly have seen the way her face had paled.

'Not yet. But I'm going to. I'll make sure of it,' her sister said determinedly.

'Bethany!' Sian turned now, her eyes wide with disapproval.

'Would you mind?' Bethany arched blonde brows questioningly.

'How do you know he's good-looking?' Sian didn't answer the question, trying to assimilate in her mind the picture of Bethany and Jarrett together. She couldn't see it at all!

'Easy,' her sister smiled. 'I vaguely remember him. And I read this magazine article about him a few months ago.'

Sian frowned. 'You never mentioned it.'

'No, well . . . To tell you the truth, Sian, I wasn't sure you would want to know. It was only a small article, and mainly about the company. But there was a lovely photograph of Jarrett along with it.'

Sian moistened her lips with the tip of her tongue. 'How—how did he look?'

'Gorgeous!' Bethany grinned dreamily. 'Really – gorgeous,' she repeated enthusiastically. 'His hair has been bleached blonder by the sun, and he has a deep, deep tan. It looks marvellous against his luminous green eyes. As for his body . . . !'

'Bethany!' Sian was deeply shocked by the desire in her sister's face, especially for a man she knew only too intimately herself.

'Well, he was wearing this pair of dark green swimming trunks—just,' Bethany added pointedly. 'And as it was a full-length photograph it didn't leave much to the imagination.'

Sian remembered that body only too well, knew what magic it could induce when you least expected it. She had known that seduction herself, and she feared for her impressionably young sister. At nineteen Bethany was still very immature in some ways. Sian knew that that was partly her fault, that she had been over-protective of her sister since their mother died, but she knew that Bethany was much too naïve to cope with the complexities of a man like Jarrett. No one woman was experienced or sophisticated enough to cope with that.

'He's too old for you, Bethany,' she said abruptly.

'Only thirty-six.' She gave Sian a sideways glance. 'You're only three years older than me, and you didn't think he was too old for you.'

To explain to Bethany that Jarrett had been the reason for her own growing-up would be to reveal too much. 'Well, I can tell you now that Daddy won't approve. Especially if he hears the way you've been talking about him!'

'You aren't going to tell him?' her sister groaned. 'I

haven't even met Jarrett yet. At least give me a chance.'

Sian very much doubted that Jarrett would be interested in Bethany; youth and naïveté were something he had sworn to stay away from when he had walked out on nineteen-year-old Sian. In many ways Bethany was even more immature than she had been three years ago, and surely wouldn't appeal to a man as jaded as Jarrett.

He sounded as if he had changed little, as if he had remained as lithe and attractive as ever. The local girls of Swannell wouldn't know what had hit them when he came back to town!

Bethany's thoughts seemed to be running along the same lines. 'Of course I'll have to get in first,' she frowned. 'I wonder where he'll stay?'

Sian served the salad and steak for lunch, putting the hot potatoes in a vegetable bowl in the centre of the table, expecting her father at any moment. He always arrived home from his accountancy office at exactly one-thirty, and she always had his lunch waiting for him.

She shrugged. 'The Swan,' she named the local hotel and public house. 'It's the only place he can stay.' Swannell didn't boast more than the one hotel, although the one they had was of a good quality. The way Jarrett had been living the last three years it would need to be to get his patronage!

'Mm, I suppose so.' Bethany chewed thoughtfully on her bottom lip.

Sian sighed. 'Did it ever occur to you that he might be bringing his wife with him?'

'Wife?' Her sister blinked her surprise. 'But he isn't married—is he?' she added uncertainly.

'How would I know?' Sian's tone was tight.

'Well, I—I just thought you might.' Bethany frowned.

'Oh, damn! You don't think he is, do you?'

'I have no idea.'

'Aren't you interested?'

Interested? In whether or not Jarrett had a wife? Once upon a time Sian would have been very interested. But not any more. Jarrett could have had a dozen wives the last three years—and with his sex drive that was possible!—and she wouldn't give a damn. She was engaged to Chris, wasn't interested in Jarrett's movements any more.

'No,' she answered flatly.

'Well, I would have thought in the circumstances—'

'Serve the steaks, Bethany,' she interrupted abruptly. 'I just heard Daddy come in.'

Their father's arrival home was a welcome interruption to what was turning out to be a painful conversation, and her smile was bright and welcoming as he came into the kitchen. He was a man in his late fifties, his hair still thick, but iron-grey, his eyes the same deep blue as Bethany's, his frame leaner than it used to be owing to a heart attack several years ago, the doctor ordering him to lose weight at the time, weight he had never regained. Sian took after her mother, the mother who had died while both girls were still at school.

'What a welcome sight for any man!' her father greeted jovially, sitting down at the table.

'Steak and salad?' Sian derided.

His smile deepened. 'No, my two beautiful daughters waiting for me when I get home. Although no one would think you were sisters. I think I'd blame you on the milk man, Bethany, if you didn't look exactly like my mother.'

It was a long-standing family joke about the difference between the two sisters, Bethany being tiny and explosive, Sian tall and cool, but they all laughed together nonetheless.

Together. Yes, they were a very 'together' family, and it was something Sian had come to treasure over the years. She had taken care of her father and Bethany since she was fourteen years old, and when she and Chris married they intended to continue living here. Chris had easily fallen in with the idea of staying in the house that was more than big enough for all of them without them tripping over each other every minute of the day.

'Sian's more likely to be the result of the milkman,' Bethany teased. 'He has red hair!'

'So he does,' their father chuckled.

Sian was used to this playful teasing, but knew that with her red hair and hazel eyes she looked exactly like her mother.

As usual lunch was a lighthearted affair, Jarrett King seemingly forgotten by Bethany for a few minutes. Their father left to return to his office at two o'clock, and Bethany disappeared upstairs once they had done the washing-up together.

Sian followed her up a few minutes later, waiting until her sister had come off the telephone before talking to her. 'Shouldn't you be getting back?' She frowned at the chaos that was her sister's bedroom, clothes and magazines strewn everywhere.

'Mm.' Bethany had a self-satisfied smile on her face, unconcerned with the mess about her. 'I just checked at the Swan. Jarrett's due there any day now.'

Sian's heart gave an unexpected lurch. So soon! Heavens, he could even turn up today. Her hunted feeling earlier while she shopped no longer seemed so far-fetched.

'Bethany, it's two-fifteen,' she reminded her sharply.

'So Gloria will have a moan at me for being late.' Her sister seemed unworried. 'She knows I'm the best stylist she has.'

'*Ex*-stylist, if you don't stop messing her about,' Sian warned. 'You were late this morning too.'

'I needed those denims. And they weren't ironed.'

'I've already told you I haven't had time to do the ironing yet—'

'Sian, don't you ever regret being a slave to Daddy and me?' Bethany frowned. 'You've been taking care of us for the last eight years, and you never moan or complain.'

Sian's smile was tight. 'I didn't realise I was a slave, I thought I did it because we're family.'

Bethany stood up to hug her. 'We are,' she smiled. 'But don't you ever feel like a break? Don't you ever want to just say "to hell with you" and just leave?'

'When you were an audacious little brat of thirteen I felt like it a lot of times,' Sian laughed as Bethany blushed. 'But I've never really considered leaving you and Daddy.' She was suddenly serious. 'Mummy—well, she expected me to take care of you both.'

'But you were only fourteen yourself. Didn't you—'

'Bethany,' she interrupted patiently, 'Gloria may be very forbearing where you're concerned—and that may be because you're her best stylist,' she mocked gently. 'But—'

'Who does your hair for you!'

'You do,' Sian laughed as her sister rose to her bait. 'But even Gloria has her breaking point. You're going to be at least half an hour late already.'

Bethany grimaced. 'And I have Mrs Jones's blue rinse to do,' she groaned.

'So much for a client's secrets!'

Her sister laughed. 'Careful, or I'll tell everyone about that grey hair I found amongst all that red last week!'

'It was blonde,' Sian pretended indignation.

'If you say so,' Bethany taunted. 'As you pulled it out we'll never know—until you get two grown back in its place, that is.'

'Get back to work!' Sian laughed.

'I'm going, I'm going,' Bethany picked up a magazine and handed it to Sian. 'I found that magazine with the article about Jarrett in,' and she hurriedly left the room, running down the stairs, and the roar of the Mini's engine soon told Sian her sister was on her way back into town.

She held the magazine in her hands for long timeless minutes without looking at it. She was afraid to look at it! And she was afraid of Bethany's single-minded interest in Jarrett; she knew better than anyone how he could hurt her young sister with his cruelty and indifference to anyone's wishes but his own.

Finally she had to look at the magazine article; she couldn't stop herself any longer, her breath catching in her throat at the familiar figure in the photograph, the long muscled legs, the lean thighs only just covered by the green bathing trunks, the taut stomach and powerful chest, the whole of his body deeply tanned, his chest covered with a fine sheen of dark blond hair. Lastly she looked at his face—a face little changed, the jaw still as determined, his mouth still as forceful, sensually so, his nose long and hawkish, jutting out below deeply green eyes surrounded by thick dark lashes, his brows the same dark blond, a startling contrast to the sun-bleached fairness of his hair. Bethany was right, Jarrett was devastating, although she wondered at the cynicism in his eyes, the lines of decadence beside his nose and mouth. He obviously hadn't spent the last three years longing for Swannell—or anyone in it.

She read the article with the picture, of how his uncle had died several months ago and he was now in complete control of the King Construction Company, of how he intended extending the company more in England.

A sudden panicky thought entered Sian's mind. Suppose he was coming to Swannell with that purpose in mind? Suppose—No, the King office in Swannell had long since closed up; Jarrett's move to America had forced that decison. He must just be coming here out of curiosity's sake, to see the town that had once been his home, the town that had been his stepping-stone to the multi-millionaire he now was.

She forced herself to read the rest of the article, getting lost in the maze of assets that King Construction had, although the cryptic comment at the end of the article puzzled her somewhat. Obviously it was one of those 'in' magazines, the type that thought you already knew the life history of its victim, and the mention of some woman called Arlette meant nothing to her. 'And while the more than attractive Mr King is in his native England, the lonely Arlette will be cooling her heels in New York as she waits for his return. If I were Mr King I would want the lovely Arlette with me!' came the reporter's personal comment.

Arlette. She didn't need to be told that this was the latest woman in Jarrett's life; it was all too obvious. She would be beautiful, of course, would have the sophistication and raw sensuality that he liked. God, that he *demanded*!

Sian threw the magazine down on the bed in disgust, going determinedly down the stairs. She had wasted enough time thinking about Jarrett for one day, she doubted he would waste a minute of his valuable time thinking of the naïve teenager he had left behind him without a qualm.

It was already after three o'clock, she would have to hurry if she was to do the housework before she went back to the surgery. She hated being rushed, and inwardly blamed Jarrett King for upsetting her routine. Everyone in Swannell knew he had made a success of his life—did he have to come back and flaunt it!

She arrived back at the surgery with only a minute to spare, smiling at Chris as he came out to speak to her. He was a very handsome man, with unruly dark curls that he kept short, laughing blue eyes that could be stormy with emotion, with a tall athletic body, and he enjoyed all sports; he and Sian often challenged each other to a game of tennis—which she usually lost.

Chris and his family had come to Swannell almost three years ago, and Chris had been in partnership with Martin Cross for most of that time. Their veterinary practice was very successful.

It had been Chris's love and gentleness with the animals he treated that had first attracted her to him, although it had taken him some time to persuade her to even go out with him. Now she wore his ring, her admiration for him having turned to love during the year they had been dating.

He bent to kiss her lightly on the lips, the door still firmly locked against the public. 'Have a good afternoon, love?'

'A bit hectic.' She put all thought of Jarrett King from her mind, feeling it was disloyal to Chris to even think of another relationship she had had in the past when she was engaged to marry him. 'And you?' she smiled.

'Fine,' he nodded, sitting on the edge of her desk. 'Feel like going out to dinner tonight?'

Her brows rose. 'What are we celebrating?'

'Nothing,' he smiled, looking boyish despite his thirty years. Sian had to resist the impulse to smooth back the unruly lock of dark hair from his forehead. 'You're looking beautiful, it's a lovely day, and I think we can afford to go out for one meal,' he teased.

She didn't dispute that fact, knew they had enough saved for several meals if they wanted them. They had been saving hard lately, allowing little for luxuries, perhaps a nice meal out was what they needed. 'I'd like that,' she agreed, smiling ruefully as the doorbell rang. 'Your first customer.' She stood up to unlock the door.

He grimaced, kissing her lightly on the mouth once again. 'Let's hope it's a nice quiet hamster to start with. They can bring the snakes in later!'

Sian was laughing as she opened the door. Several weeks ago the local zoo had made an urgent call to Chris about one of their reptiles, and when he got there he found it was a boa constrictor! She had a feeling he regretted being on call to the zoo after that visit.

The next couple of hours passed quickly, with a constant stream of cats and dogs and rabbits needing Chris and Martin's expert attention—but no snakes, thank goodness! For Sian her time at work always passed with high speed, mainly because no two days were the same and because she enjoyed what she was doing.

It was seven-thirty before she and Chris were ready to leave, Chris driving to her home so that she could change her clothes for going out. Chris came into the house with her, and went straight into the lounge to sit with her father, the two men getting along with an easy familiarity.

Bethany was on the telephone when Sian reached the top of the stairs, and she gave Sian a startled look before ringing off and following Sian into her bedroom. 'You're early,' she frowned.

'It's almost eight,' she shrugged.

'Oh,' her sister gave a light laugh, 'in that case you're late. I—er—Are you staying in this evening?'

'No, as a matter of fact I'm going out.' Sian gave Bethany a sharp look. 'You aren't bringing Jeremy here again, are you?' she frowned. 'You know Daddy can't stand him.'

'Jeremy and I broke up ages ago,' her sister dismissed impatiently. 'Well, at least a week ago,' she amended ruefully. 'No, I just wondered because I'm going out too.'

'And?'

'I—Could I borrow your black blouse?' Bethany asked breathlessly. 'It looks really good with my grey velvet trousers. You aren't going to wear it, are you?' she added hopefully.

'No.' Sian laughingly threw the blouse to her sister. 'Thank goodness I'm taller than you and so none of my dresses fit you, otherwise you'd be borrowing all of my clothes!'

Bethany stood up to leave, looking a little hurt. 'You can borrow anything of mine you want.'

'Not tonight,' she refused, her sister's taste in fashion tending to be a little too young for her, her own style tending to be smart and well-tailored rather than strictly fashionable. 'Have a good time,' and she hurried to use the bathroom first.

'You too,' Bethany said absently.

Sian had no doubt about enjoying herself. Chris was always good company, and the food at the Raven restaurant was excellent without being too much of a strain on the pocket. It was a quietly intimate restaurant, only holding about forty people, exactly the sort of place to go to unwind after a busy day.

'I'm glad I suggested this,' Chris said as they waited for their meal to be served. He was obviously starting to relax now, his hand holding hers across the width of the table.

'So am I,' she smiled at him warmly, wondering how she could have been so lucky as to have a man as gentle and considerate as Chris fall in love with her. He looked so handsome in the navy blue suit and light blue shirt, his skin lightly tanned, and she knew that many women would envy her escort.

But for the moment her attention was riveted on the man standing at the doorway. And well it might! Jarrett hadn't changed at all, was still a powerful presence, an aura of arrogance and assurance emanating from him, even the casualness of his clothes, the black fitted trousers and dark green shirt making him stand out as a man alone.

But he was far from alone! Standing at his side, looking very beautiful, was Bethany!

Sian's eyes widened as she saw the way her sister clung to Jarrett's arm, the way she gazed up at him with adoring eyes, and she knew Jarrett had made a conquest. An easy one, if Bethany's bemused expression was anything to go by.

Finally she forced herself to look back at Jarrett, and felt a jolt go through her body as she found green eyes fixed on her in total recognition. For timeless seconds their gazes locked as they stared at each other, Sian seeing the way Jarrett's eyes darkened in colour, his mouth curving into a smile, an intimately enticing smile that three years ago would have had her running impetuously into his waiting arms.

But that was three years ago; she had Chris now! With a cool nod of recognition, she deliberately broke her gaze from Jarrett's and turned away; the mystery of how Bethany came to be with Jarrett when this afternoon she hadn't so much as spoken to him could be answered by her sister later. But she had a feeling her sister wasn't going to come out of it favourably.

'Chris, I—'

'Sian, how are you?'

Not even his voice had changed, still deep and slightly husky, completely confident, nothing hesitant about this man at all.

She turned slowly, willing herself to meet Jarrett's gaze unflinchingly. He towered over their table, lean and attractive, deep lines of experience etched into his face, a wariness to his eyes as he looked steadily down at her.

She swallowed hard, her hand unconsciously clutching tighter to Chris's, although she was unaware of his sharp look. 'I'm well, thank you, Jarrett.' Her voice came out cool and composed—much to her surprise. This was all like some horrendous dream, and she was surprised she could talk at all.

'Good,' he said with satisfaction. 'You've grown into a beautiful woman, Sian,' he added huskily before turning to Chris. 'I'm pleased to meet you, Mr . . . ?' he looked enquiringly at the other man.

Chris stood up. 'Newman, Christopher Newman,' he supplied, politely shaking the other man's extended hand, his expression a little wary as he eyed him curiously.

'My fiancé,' Sian put in pointedly—and then wondered why she needed to challenge Jarrett in this way. What possible interest could it be to him what Chris meant to her, or what part he played in her life?

'Indeed?' Jarrett drawled, the expression in his eyes hidden now, his lids hooded. 'I had heard that you were engaged, Sian. When is the wedding?'

She paled at the look of fierce anger in his face, unable to answer him. She couldn't have spoken if her life had depended on it, her tongue seeming cleaved to the roof of her mouth. She looked at Chris appealingly.

'Next month,' she heard him answer Jarrett. 'Just four more weeks and Sian will be my wife,' he added with satisfaction.

The anger in Jarrett's eyes threatened to flare out of control. And Sian knew why. She had just four weeks to go before she and Chris married, when three years ago she should have married Jarrett!

CHAPTER TWO

THIS man should have been her husband, and if he hadn't chosen to join his uncle in America when he did he probably would be. But would he? Jarrett looked as if he enjoyed the freedom and power his new wealth gave him, and if he looked a little jaded that was his business. Although she would take a guess at a woman being involved—there always had been!—possibly the Arlette the magazine had referred to so pointedly. Why *hadn't* he brought the other woman with him?

Maybe, as with her, he preferred to leave the current woman in his life at home, to forget about her while he found someone else to amuse him. And it looked as if that 'someone else' was going to be Bethany!'

Her sister had been sixteen when Sian had been dating Jarrett, and at the time he had treated Bethany like a troublesome child. That hadn't been surprising. Bethany had always wanted to tag along with him, never left them alone for a minute when they were in the house, and at thirty-three Jarrett had already been highly sensual, his passion surpassing any other man's she had ever known. Bethany had cramped his style, but now it seemed she was old enough to be at the receiving end of that fiery desire that had so unnerved Sian three years ago. In those days, when she was alone with Jarrett, she hadn't been able to control her response to him, and she now feared that mindless obsession for Bethany.

Not that her sister looked as if it frightened her; she

was clinging unashamedly to his arm, small and kitten-ish, unaware of the leashed danger in the man standing at her side, at the devastation he could wreak in a woman's life before he walked away without so much as a backward glance.

As he had with her! Oh, she had loved him so much then, would have done anything for him. But her unreserved love hadn't been enough for him.

'Darling?'

She looked almost dazedly at Chris, seeing his puzzled frown. 'Sorry?' she said jerkily.

'Mr King was offering us his congratulations.'

'Really?' She turned to look at Jarrett, unable to read his reaction now. His expression was deliberately bland, the fierce anger gone.

It was an anger he had had no right to feel in the first place! She had waited for him to come back to her, had waited a long slow lifetime for him to come back, but he never had. He had no right to feel anything about the fact that she was marrying another man.

'But of course,' he drawled now. 'Why don't you join Bethany and me and we can have a celebration dinner on your behalf?'

'That's very—'

'No!' Sian's sharp denial interrupted Chris, and she flushed as Jarrett's eyes narrowed to hard green pebbles, not even daring to look at Chris for his reaction to her outburst. Poor Chris must be wondering what on earth was going on! 'We've already started our meal,' she added more calmly, indicating the half-eaten melon on their plates.

Jarrett shrugged. 'You could easily transfer to our table. It would be no trouble, I'm sure.' He made it sound as if he would *make* sure it wasn't!

'Can't you see that they would rather be alone, Jarrett?' Bethany cooed up at him. 'They probably have plans for the wedding to discuss.'

Green eyes narrowed at this suggestion, and once again Sian was given the impression that the idea of her marriage to Chris displeased him.

'We do have the reception to talk about,' she confirmed firmly, undaunted by that displeasure. 'And we wouldn't want to bore you with the details.'

'I'm sure I wouldn't be bored.' Jarrett's voice was hard, his eyes challenging as he once more met her gaze. 'I've had some practice at it myself,' he added softly.

Colour heightened her cheeks before quickly fading again. 'It can be a tiring business,' she told him stiltedly. 'Especially if it turns out to be unnecessary.'

What reply Jarrett would have made to that deliberate taunt she never knew. 'Our table is ready, Jarrett,' came Bethany's timely interruption.

His mouth tightened, then he gave a slow nod. 'Very well,' he said slowly. 'It was good to see you again, Sian. Newman,' he nodded abrupt dismissal of the other man.

Chris slowly sat down as the other couple moved to their table across the room, Bethany's face animated as she spoke to the preoccupied man sitting across from her. 'So that's Jarrett King,' he muttered.

Sian's eyes widened at the open dislike in her fiancé's voice. 'Yes, that's Jarrett,' she said in a puzzled voice, wondering at Chris's attitude. Apart from that curt departure Jarrett had been very polite. And yet Chris seemed to dislike him on sight, an unusual reaction for him. Chris seemed to get along with everyone usually. Obviously not Jarrett.

'He isn't what I expected at all,' he mumbled, a frown to his dark blue eyes.

'Expected?' she echoed sharply.

He shrugged. 'Everyone in Swannell has heard of the famous Jarrett King.' He glanced over at the other couple. 'I'm not sure Bethany should be with a man like him. I've heard things about Jarrett King that make him highly unsuitable as a companion for Bethany.'

Sian had stiffened now, for some reason resenting the same criticism she herself had directed at him mentally. 'Really?'

'She's too young to handle a piranha like him—'

'I think that's going a little too far, Chris,' she protested heatedly.

His eyes narrowed, his mouth tight. 'Why are you defending the man?'

She shook her head. 'I'm not defending him—'

'No?' he bit out angrily. 'It sounds very much that way to me.' He eyed her moodily.

She was very much aware of Bethany and Jarrett as they sat across the room from them, of Bethany's sparkling charm and Jarrett's lazy humour, almost as if Bethany's efforts to charm him amused rather than attracted him.

Her mouth was tight as she turned back to Chris. 'I agree with you that he is totally unsuitable for Bethany,' her tone was abrupt, 'but I don't agree that he's a piranha.'

His eyes flashed deeply. 'Not even after the way he walked out on you?' he rasped.

All the colour drained from Sian's face, leaving her eyes looking huge and haunted. 'What do you know about that?' she choked, crumbling the bread roll on her plate to destruction.

Chris's mouth twisted. 'Only what the people in this town felt I should know when we became engaged.'

She swallowed hard, having no idea he had been told the gossip about her. 'Then perhaps they told you wrong!'

'He left with another woman, didn't he?' Chris scorned.

'Yes.' Her voice was pained at the truth of that.

'Let's eat, Sian,' he muttered as their main course arrived. 'This is hardly the place for this discussion.'

She didn't think anywhere would be the right place for discussing what was basically a private matter between herself and Jarrett. He had left with Nina Marshall, yes, but only because he found more pleasure in being with her than with Sian.

All enjoyment in the meal had gone for her. All she was aware of was Chris's brooding anger, and Jarrett and Bethany's obvious enjoyment in each other's company, the sound of Jarrett's husky laughter beginning to grate on her nerves by the time they got to the coffee stage of their meal, and she refused any of the strong brew, as did Chris.

'Shall we go?' he asked tersely.

She had never seen Chris like this before; she was more used to his easy charm and gentleness. This side of him was completely new to her, and she wondered if jealousy of Jarrett could have prompted this reaction. She could have told him he had no reason to feel anything over Jarrett; any love she might have felt for him had died when Nina Marshall returned to Swannell, also dismissed from his life. In time she could have perhaps forgiven his loving the other woman more than her, but when Nina returned a couple of weeks later without him it became obvious that neither of them had meant that much to Jarrett.

As they walked past Jarrett's table his hand came out

to grasp Sian's wrist. She looked down with a gasp; Chris had gone on ahead to pay the bill and so not witnessed this intimacy. But Bethany had, and her embarrassment was all the more acute because of her sister's wide-eyed stare.

'Let go of me,' she ordered between gritted teeth, very conscious of her hip pressed against his arm, could feel the warmth of his body through his shirt.

He made no effort to release her, his thumb moving rhythmically against the delicate veins in her wrist. 'I have to talk to you,' he told her throatily, his eyes intent.

'I'm sorry,' she wrenched her arm out of his grasp. 'If you'll excuse me . . . ?'

'No!' He stood up, towering over her as he always had, as powerfully built as ever. 'Sian, I need to talk to you.' He clasped her forearms.

'Why?' she asked flatly. 'Isn't it a little late for talking between us? I thought we'd said it all three years ago.'

'Sian—'

'Darling, are you ready to leave?' Chris had paid the bill, coming back for her as he realised she hadn't followed him out, and his irritation fanned to anger as he saw the way Jarrett was touching her. 'If you wouldn't mind, King . . .' He pulled Sian to his side, a reckless challenge on his face. 'It may have escaped your notice,' he added tauntingly, 'but Sian wears *my* ring now.'

She gasped at this deliberate provocation, seeing Jarrett's eyes narrow to steely slits.

'Sian never wore my ring,' he answered in a mild voice—too mild! 'We never needed such affectations as rings to know she belonged to me.'

Sian felt herself sway, forcing herself to remain standing as Chris's hand crushed hers. But she couldn't speak, knowing she would choke if she even attempted it.

Chris was white with fury. 'Well, she doesn't belong to you now,' he snapped. 'So just stay away from her!'

Jarrett's jaw had tightened ominously at this, a pulse beating steadily there. 'I'll stay away from Sian if she tells me to—and if I think she really means it,' he added tauntingly. 'So don't give me orders, Newman,' he grated. 'Sian could tell you—only too well—how much better I respond to—persuasion.'

'Why, you—'

'Could we please leave, Chris?' Sian had finally found her voice; this last provocation had been too much. She looked at Jarrett with cold hazel eyes. 'And I do ask you to stay away from me, Jarrett—as I ask you to stay away from Bethany.'

Her sister coloured painfully, her embarrassment acute. 'Sian, you can't—'

'I agree, she can't,' Jarrett drawled, bestowing a smouldering smile on the besotted Bethany. 'And you didn't mean that, Sian,' he looked back at her with mocking eyes. 'I always knew when you were telling the truth—and that wasn't it.'

Her mouth twisted, her hand through the crook of Chris's arm now. 'How unfortunate I was never as perceptive where you were concerned,' she was deliberately insulting, 'then I would have known from the first what sort of man you are.'

'And that is?' he bit out harshly, all amusement gone now.

'The sort of man I don't like dating my sister!' She turned away from the angry flame of his eyes. 'I'll talk to you later, Bethany,' she warned.

Her sister looked sulky. 'I'm not a child, Sian,' she snapped.

'I agree—you aren't,' Sian said tightly. 'Which is precisely the reason I think we should talk.'

'Still trying to be the conscience of your whole family, Sian?' Jarrett derided.

She looked at him coldly. 'Still *caring* for my family, yes, Jarrett. But caring is something you know nothing about. Excuse us.' This time she and Chris managed to get out of the restaurant undisturbed.

'Arrogant bastard!' Chris rasped as he opened the car door for her to get in, closing it with a decisive slam.

Sian knew how disturbed he had been by the encounter by the fact that he swore; Chris never used strong language. But about this she couldn't blame him. She could quite cheerfully have sworn herself!

Jarrett *was* arrogant, more so than ever before. And he was out to cause trouble. Why, she had no idea; he had hurt her badly enough in the past without wanting to cause a strain between herself and Chris. But the strain was already there, with Chris driving recklessly back to her home.

'I'm coming inside.' There was a determined glitter to his eyes. 'We need to talk.'

She could see that, knew that Chris deserved some sort of explanation. But about tonight she didn't have one; she had no idea why Jarrett was acting as he was, had no idea what he was doing back in Swannell. He was a little young to be retracing his roots!

Her father was still up when they got in, so she went and made them all a cup of coffee, giving a barely perceptible shrug of her shoulders to Chris, seeing by the stubborn set of his mouth that he intended staying as long as it took for her father to go to bed. He was determined to have that talk with her tonight.

Sian felt totally confused as she prepared the coffee.

She had no idea why Jarrett should want to talk to her about anything – especially while he was dating her sister! She couldn't let Bethany be hurt as she had been hurt, she had to protect her sister against herself if it came to it.

'Have a nice evening?' Her father took the cup of coffee she handed him, oblivious of the strained atmosphere between the engaged couple.

'We went to the Raven.' Sian avoided giving him a direct answer, the reputation of the restaurant such that he was sure to think they had enjoyed themselves.

'You didn't happen to see Bethany, did you?' he enquired casually.

'We—'

'You know the Raven isn't her sort of place,' she interrupted Chris's reply, knowing by his angry scowl that he was about to say more than she wanted him to. But again she had avoided telling a deliberate lie. The Raven *wasn't* Bethany's sort of place.

'No,' her father chuckled, very comfortable and relaxed in his casual and old trousers and tattered worn cardigan, his usual attire after his formal clothing of the day at his office. 'She's more likely to be at the Swan, they have a discothèque there.'

'Not on a Wednesday,' Sian told him absently, aware of Chris's glowering impatience.

'Oh well, I suppose she's just out with one of her friends,' her father shrugged. 'She left in such a hurry she didn't have time to tell me. I doubt she'll be too late.'

'No,' again Sian answered, when it became obvious Chris was going to make no effort at conversation.

'There was a good Western on television tonight,' her father told her happily. 'I enjoyed that.'

Sian smiled indulgently, Westerns were her father's

passion. 'John Wayne?' she teased, knowing the Duke was her father's favourite cowboy.

'Randolph Scott,' he named his second favourite, and put down his empty cup. 'Well, I'm off to bed now. I'll see you tomorrow, I suppose, Chris?' he smiled at the other man. Liking and respect existed between the two of them, a deep contrast to what her father had felt for Jarrett; he had never quite trusted him. And that mistrust had been justified!

'I'm sure you will, George.' Chris roused himself enough to be polite.

Sian stood up to kiss her father affectionately goodnight, a habit from when she was a child, a pleasant habit. 'See you in the morning,' she smiled.

'Mm,' he touched her cheek. 'And don't be too late to bed,' he frowned. 'You're looking a little peaky today.'

'Pre-wedding nerves,' she joked.

Her father smiled. 'Both of you, by the look of it,' he teased Chris's tense expression.

'It's a hectic time,' Chris mumbled.

'I agree,' her father laughed. 'But it will soon be over, and I'm sure the honeymoon will be worth it,' he added with a mischievous twinkle in his eye.

'Dad!'

He could still be heard chuckling as he went up to his bedroom, having no idea of the fraught tension he had left behind him, sure that they would be in each other's arms the moment he left the room.

'Is there still going to be a wedding?' Chris finally rasped. 'Or a honeymoon, for that matter?'

Sian gave him a startled look, paling. 'What do you mean?'

He stood up forcefully, as if the inactivity of sitting

down made him impatient. 'Don't try telling me that meeting King again hasn't unsettled you,' he scorned.

'I found it a little—strange,' she chose her words carefully, 'but that's all.'

'Is it?' he derided. 'Then why didn't you want your father told that Bethany was out with him?'

She sighed, chewing on her inner lip. 'He wouldn't understand—'

'Neither do I! God, when I think of the way he was touching you! I could have hit him in that moment,' Chris growled.

She had known that, but if he had Jarrett would have hit him back, and he wouldn't have pulled his punches either. Jarrett was a physical man in every way, and he would have derived enjoyment from hitting Chris.

'I didn't like it either—'

'Didn't you?' he ground out. 'You didn't exactly look as if you were fighting him off when I came back to see what was delaying you!'

'We were in a public restaurant,' she flushed. 'I didn't want to make a scene. As for my father being told about Bethany—he doesn't like Jarrett, he never did. It would upset him to know Bethany was out with him.'

'And you think it didn't upset me to see King touching you?' Chris asked bitterly.

'I can see it did,' she soothed, her hand on his arm. 'But I didn't choose to have him touch me.'

'What did he want?'

'To talk to me—'

'Talk!' he derided harshly. 'It looked to me as if talking were the last thing he had on his mind. The man was eating you with his eyes! Tell me about him, Sian, tell me about the two of you, why you broke up.'

She turned away. 'We just weren't suited.'

'He doesn't give that impression,' Chris said dryly. 'In fact, he seemed to imply you were very suited, in some ways,' he looked at her searchingly.

She closed her eyes, flashes of vivid memory going in and out of her mind—she and Jarrett swimming in the river together, making love afterwards on a blanket beneath the willow tree, its weeping branches affording them a privacy that hid them from the outside world. After that first magical time together they had spent a lot of summer afternoons in the same way, never tiring of each other, never quite sated as they longed for the next time they could be alone together to make love.

'You were lovers!' Chris rasped at her silence.

She raised her lashes. 'I told you there'd been some-one else—'

'But not *him*!' Chris groaned.

The flecks of green in her hazel eyes were more noticeable as her anger rose at the disgust in his face. 'Why shouldn't it have been him? I was going to marry him!'

'Why didn't you?'

'Circumstances,' she revealed tautly.

Chris's eyes narrowed to stormy blue pools. 'The woman Nina Marshall,' he demanded to know.

Sian moistened her lips with the tip of her tongue, looking down at her clasped hands. 'Yes. He went to America, I decided not to go with him.'

'Tell me about it.'

'Chris—'

'Just tell me, Sian,' he sighed his impatience. 'Don't I have a right to know about you and him?'

'I—I suppose so.' She swallowed hard, sitting down, knowing it wouldn't be easy to relive the memories. 'I was nineteen when I met Jarrett. Oh, I'd seen him about town, but he was a little too old for me, a little out of my league, so we'd never actually spoken. He ran a branch of his uncle's business here, had a steady girl-friend called—called Nina,' she revealed painfully. 'He and I met one day, quite by accident, at Mrs Day's.' Her expression was far away, vividly remembering that first meeting with Jarrett, the jolt of awareness that had seemed to shoot through both of them the moment their eyes met. 'He—he had some men doing some work at her house, an extension, I think. And I—I'd taken some apples round from the orchard here. He was there talking to his men, we began to talk, and—'

'And so he dropped his girl-friend and started going out with you,' Chris derided.

Sian flushed. 'Not exactly. He told me things had been cooling between him and Nina for some time, meeting me just ended it sooner than it would have done. That's what he said,' she insisted at Chris's contemptuous expression.

'The man would have said anything to get you!'

'Perhaps,' she avoided his glance. 'But at the time I believed him. We spent an idyllic summer together, and after two months he asked me to marry him. I accepted,' she continued softly. 'We'd already started planning the wedding when his uncle invited him out to run the American business.'

'You didn't want to go?'

She gave him a sharp look. 'He was going to be my husband, of course I would have gone.'

'But he went to America without you.'

'Yes.'

'Why?'

'Because by that time he was back with Nina,' she said shrilly.

'What happened to her?' Chris frowned. 'He seems to be very much on his own now.'

He seemed to be, but the magazine article implied differently; Arlette was now the woman in his life. 'Nina Marshall lives in London now, with her husband,' she told Chris dully.

'So she wasn't stupid enough to marry him either.'

Sian stiffened. 'I believe it was Jarrett's decision not to marry.'

'He seems to make a habit of it!'

'Yes.' She didn't dispute what was fact, she knew just how selfish Jarrett could be.

'Do you still love him?' Chris had calmed down a little now and was more his gentle self.

'No,' she answered with certainty. 'My love for him died a long time ago.'

Chris came over to put his arms about her, drawing her into the comfort of his arms. 'Do you still love me?' he asked teasingly.

She gave him a warm smile. 'You know I do.'

He rested his forehead against hers; he was only a couple of inches taller than her. 'I love you too. I just found it strange being confronted with your last fiancé.'

'You make it sound as if I've had hundreds!' she derided. 'And as Jarrett said, we were never officially engaged. I doubt he ever meant to go through with marrying me, even if he and Nina hadn't—well, if they hadn't got back together.' She rested against Chris's shoulder. 'I was young, and naïve, and easily impressed by his maturity and experience. A bit like hundreds of other girls of that age. You don't realise until it's too late that you were just another conquest, a conquest to be made in any way possible, even with an offer of marriage.'

She spoke quietly, bitterly, aware that she wasn't telling the whole truth, not to Chris or herself. Jarrett's offer of marriage had been genuine, as had been his love for her; he couldn't possibly have pretended the way he trembled with the emotion, he was usually a man of strength and determination. But she hadn't been enough for him, and he had ultimately returned to the more sophisticated Nina. Finding out that the other woman still featured very much in his life had been a humiliating and painful experience, one she had never forgotten.

'I'm sorry I put you through all that, darling,' Chris smoothed her hair. 'I was mad to think you could still think anything of him after the way he treated you.'

Sian didn't answer, aware that she would be telling a lie if she did. She wasn't indifferent to Jarrett. She didn't love him, but she wasn't indifferent to him either. When he had touched her at the restaurant she had felt that familiar quicksilver excitement that had been a fundamental part of their relationship; she could feel it now if she closed her eyes and thought about him.

But that was something she was trying not to do, and she returned Chris's kiss with more than their usually restrained passion, seeking oblivion from the burning ache in her body, and knowing it wasn't going to happen. She had no doubt of Chris's desire for her, could feel that desire for her now, but they had agreed to wait until they were married before making love. She knew that no matter what the provocation Chris would never break that agreement.

Although tonight he came very close to it! 'Sian darling . . . !' he groaned against her bared breasts, shuddering against her before refastening her clothes without haste or embarrassment. 'I wish it were our wedding night,' he said huskily, his dark curls ruffled from her caressing hands, his face still taut with desire. 'Then I wouldn't have to leave you like this—or myself either,' he added ruefully.

In a way Sian was glad he did have to leave, knowing that tonight his lovemaking, which she had always enjoyed, had been a substitute for more heated caresses, more experienced hands, hands that knew all the pleasure spots of her body as if by instinct.

God, she wished Jarrett had never come back, wished she never had to see him again. But there was no reason why she should; she couldn't be forced into meeting him. Although the determination in Jarrett's eyes when he told her he wanted to talk to her seemed to deny that. Jarrett King had always been very adept at getting what he wanted from life. And for some reason he wanted to talk to her.

Chris stood up, tucking his loosened shirt into his trousers before pulling on his jacket. 'Try and talk some sense into Bethany, hmm?' he said grimly. 'She really shouldn't get involved with a man like King.'

'No.' Sian stood up too, walking with him to the door.

'I'm sorry, darling.' Chris gently touched her cheek. 'I'm sure that when you thought yourself in love with him that he wasn't the hard bastard he seems now. But the way he was tonight he can only be bad for Bethany.'

'I've already said I'll talk to her,' she said stiffly.

'Sian—'

'It's very late, Chris,' her voice softened, knowing he was only showing concern for her sister, 'and I'm tired.'

'Of course you are,' he nodded, bending to kiss her lightly on the lips. 'I'll see you in the morning, darling.'

She went back to the lounge after he had left and cleared away the coffee tray, washing the cups and saucers as a way of occupying herself while she waited for Bethany to come home. The talk with her sister would be better taking place tonight, even though she wasn't looking forward to it. Bethany could be very determined when she set her mind on something, and her attraction to Jarrett seemed to be very strong.

Chris had been wrong about one thing. Jarrett had been a hard bastard three years ago too, although at the time, like Bethany now, she had been too fascinated by him to realise what he was like.

A few days before her wedding to him she had learnt exactly what sort of man he was; she had refused to even think of marrying him then and going to America with him. And yet she had still clung to some stupid belief that what she had seen had been a mistake, that her own eyes had deceived her. The day Jarrett left Swannell with Nina Marshall she had known it was the end as far as they were concerned.

And now Bethany was out with him. Her young sister couldn't have forgotten their father's fury when Jarrett had let Sian down so selfishly, or the pain he had caused Sian. She had to be made to see that he would only hurt her too. And preferably before their father learnt that she was seeing him!

It was almost twelve when she heard the sound of a powerful engine roaring to a stop outside the house, guessing Jarrett still had a liking for fast cars; he had had a Jaguar sports-car three years ago. He had been rich enough in those days, the firm he ran for his uncle was very successful, but being head of the King Construction Company had made him into a multi-millionaire; he probably drove a Ferrari or Lamborghini now!

The front door closed softly as Bethany let herself into the house, and Sian was drying her hands from washing up as she went out to meet her young sister, her voice a soft whisper so that they didn't disturb their father. 'Bethany, I—' the words lodged in her throat as she saw the man standing confidently at Bethany's side. Jarrett!

She was sure her face lost some of its colour. To see him here in her home again, after all this time! She glanced nervously up the stairs, although there was no sound from her father's room.

Jarrett's mouth twisted derisively as he saw that worried glance. 'Shall we go into the lounge?' He led the way with a confidence that spoke of past familiarity, his welcome assured then.

But it wasn't now! Dear God, did Bethany have *no* sense? It seemed not; her sister still had that dreamy enthralled look in her eyes.

Jarrett seated himself in an armchair with a confidence that knew no limits, resting the ankle of one leg on the knee of the other, his gaze steady and assured as he looked up at the two standing women.

'I—er—I invited Jarrett in for coffee.' Bethany at least seemed compelled to talk.

'Really?' Sian said stiffly, having no intention of going to bed and leaving Jarrett alone down here with her sister. She remembered too many occasions in the past when she and Jarrett had been stretched out side by side on that sofa, their lovemaking silent but impassioned while her father and sister slept on unaware upstairs.

Jarrett's gaze was narrowed on her face, his brows raised questioningly as her thoughts made her blush. 'I suggest you go and make that coffee, Bethany,' he said deeply. 'For three.'

'None for me,' Sian refused abruptly. 'It's getting rather late, Bethany,' she added pointedly.

Her sister flushed resentfully. 'Jarrett?'

'I'd like coffee,' he drawled challengingly.

With a defiant look in Sian's direction Bethany went off to the kitchen.

Sian was very conscious of being completely alone with Jarrett, of him sitting only a few feet away. And she didn't like it, she had a feeling of being manoeuvred.

'Your fiancé has gone?' he asked softly.

She kept her face stiffly averted. 'Yes.'

'He knew about us.' It was a statement, not a question.

'Yes.'

Jarrett stood up, at once seeming predatory, and Sian took a wary step backwards. His mouth twisted derisively. 'I never needed to use force on you, Sian,' he drawled mockingly.

'You would now,' she snapped.

'If I were interested,' he watched with satisfaction as she paled, 'and I am,' he added softly. 'I telephoned you earlier tonight, as soon as I got to town, but you weren't at home,' he told her huskily, suddenly very near, the heat of his body, the seduction of his aftershave, reaching out to her.

Sian refused to look at him. 'Why on earth would you telephone me?' she asked jerkily.

Suddenly he was more than just close, he was dangerously so, the lean length of his body curving into the back of her as his arms came about her waist and pulled her into him. 'Guess,' he murmured throatily against her earlobe.

CHAPTER THREE

SHE couldn't stand it, couldn't bear his proximity. Her legs felt weak, her heart was beating a wild tattoo against her rib-cage, her breathing so shallow she hardly breathed at all.

She felt his hands slowly start to move towards her breasts, and with a strong tug she moved quickly away from him, putting some distance between them as she stood behind a chair, seeing Jarrett's eyes gleam with mockery at the gesture; no chair would save her from him if he wanted her back in his arms. He made no effort to do so.

'I can guess all too easily,' she snapped.

'I doubt it.' His eyes were narrowed.

'Oh, but I can,' Sian scorned. 'You wanted a woman to keep you company your first evening back in Swannell. I'm only too pleased Bethany could accommodate you.'

'You aren't pleased at all,' he mocked. 'And it would have been you I took out to dinner if you'd been at home when I telephoned.'

'How fortunate for me that I wasn't here! And for you too. You see, I would have refused to go anywhere with you.' And she had a sneaking suspicion that she had been at home for at least part of Jarrett's conversation with Bethany, remembering the haste with which her sister had ended her telephone call when Sian had got in from work.

Her sister needn't have worried, she certainly

wouldn't have accepted an invitation from Jarrett. But if she had known Bethany had she would have tried to prevent her seeing him. Maybe her sister had known that, and felt it wiser to keep silent about the call. She had a feeling that was nearer the truth.

'I trust my sister has been suitably impressed,' she said contemptuously. 'But of course she has—you made sure of that. You can switch your charm on and off like a tap when it suits you to,' she recalled bitterly. 'Only I have no intention of standing back and letting you hurt my sister.'

'The way I hurt you,' he finished hardly.

'Exactly,' she snapped, gold flecks shining deeply in her hazel eyes.

'And how about the way you hurt me?' he rasped coldly. 'Or don't we talk about that?'

'Hurt you?' she derided scornfully. 'You can't be hurt, Jarrett. Only people with feelings and emotions can be hurt. And you don't have either!'

His face showed he was blazingly angry, his mouth a thin taut line. 'And you don't have an ounce of trust in your body,' he ground out. 'If you had you would have believed me about Nina Marshall three years ago!'

She turned away. 'I don't want to talk about it.'

'You never did,' he wrenched her round roughly. 'And because of my damned pride I didn't see why I should keep explaining myself to you.' His eyes glittered down at her like twin jewels. 'Has your distrust kept you warm at night, Sian? Has it told you it loves you? Has it made love to you until your head spins? Has it done any of *that*?'

She paled more with each groaned taunt, and turned away, refusing to listen to any more of this torture.

But Jarrett would have none of that, his fingers biting

into her arm as he made her listen to him. 'Because my pride hasn't given me any of that, Sian—'

'I'm sure your women have!' she dismissed coldly. 'As Chris has me.'

Jarrett's face darkened with an ugliness she had thought never to see again, his mouth twisted with fury, his eyes two shafts of burning light as they blazed down at her in total anger. 'Is he your lover?' he ground out.

She flushed. 'I don't see what that has to do with you,' she challenged.

'Don't you?' he returned softly, dangerously. 'If his body has mated with yours—and I refuse to call it making love,' he added harshly at her gasp of outrage. '*I* made love to you,' he claimed arrogantly. 'No other man could ever do that.'

'You arrogant—'

He sighed, shaking his head at her vehemence. 'A person can only find that true oneness with another person once in a lifetime. We both know that we were that for each other, and no amount of denial on your part can change that.'

'Then it's a pity you didn't realise it at the time!'

'I did,' he bit out. 'You didn't. *Has* Newman been to bed with you? If he has I'll kill him!'

Sian gasped at the coldness of the statement. Jarrett's face was devoid of expression—and she knew that he meant every word. This man was dangerous. 'You—'

'Sorry I was so long with the coffee.' Bethany came into the room. 'The percolator broke down, and it took me ages to realise the fuse had gone. I—' she had looked up from carrying the tray, her chatter coming to a stop as she saw the tension on the faces of the two people in front of her.

Sian saw her sister's face tighten with suspicion, the blue eyes narrowing, and she forced her own expression to be her one of usual cool confidence. 'Did you find another fuse?' She went forward to take the tray out of Bethany's hands, putting it down on the coffee-table.

'Eventually.' Bethany was still a little uncertain about what had been going on in her absence, frowning slightly.

'You didn't take the one out of the iron again, did you?' Sian teased, aware that Jarrett's hands were slowly unclenching at his sides as he regained control, his face relaxing into its usual lazy amusement.

'No.' Bethany still watched them intently. 'I found the new ones you'd put in the drawer.'

'Good,' Sian smiled. 'Are you going to pour the coffee, Bethany?' she asked lightly. 'I'm sure Jarrett is dying for a cup.'

He was completely under control now, smiling his most charming smile at the more susceptible Bethany. 'Black, no sugar,' he requested huskily.

Bethany gave him a provocative smile. 'The same for me. I brought you a cup too, Sian,' she looked at her. 'Would you like some?'

Sian wanted to go to bed, to forget all about Jarrett King for a few hours of oblivion, and most of all she wanted to forget the conversation she had just had with him. He had seemed to be implying that she was part of the reason he was back in Swannell, that he wanted to continue their relationship where it had left off three years ago.

Never! It had taken her two years to pick up the pieces of her life the last time he had destroyed her; she wasn't going to let him do it again. And he would do it; he was the type of man who needed more than one woman in his life. He already had Bethany and the absent Arlette, and now he wanted her too!

'Yes, please,' she accepted the coffee, determined to stay down here as long as she could and so lessen the time Jarrett and Bethany spent alone together.

Jarrett's gaze moved to the sofa in silent mockery as he seemed to read her thoughts, and she gave him a look of cold dislike. This man forgot nothing!

'Will you be in Swannell long, Jarrett?' she asked as they all sipped their coffee.

He shrugged. 'That depends.'

'On what?' Her eyes narrowed.

'Jarrett has put in a bid to build the new shopping centre and hotel,' Bethany told her smugly. 'So if he's the one to get the building contract—'

'Oh, I will be,' he drawled confidently.

'Then he'll be here for some time,' Bethany beamed her satisfaction of that idea.

'Yes,' Sian realised hollowly, having no idea Jarrett's was one of the three companies to put in for that contract. No one had mentioned it before now. Or perhaps none of the town council had actually realised King Construction Company *was* Jarrett King. Most of them were too old to know their *own* name! 'Surely a contract like that is rather small to deal with yourself, Jarrett? I thought you had gone on to bigger and better things.' Her sarcasm was unmistakeable.

'I have,' he snapped. 'But I couldn't resist the idea of coming back here. It's nice to see old friends again,' he taunted softly. 'And make new ones,' he smiled at Bethany.

Bethany gave a coy smile as he openly flirted with her. 'You knew me before, Jarrett.'

'But you weren't a friend then, were you?' he said throatily.

God, the man was a monster! He was deliberately attracting Bethany, and Sian wasn't naïve enough to think he was doing it to spite her. He was enjoying the flirtation, damn him!

'So you intend building one of those concrete monstrosities in town,' she heard herself scorn.

The green eyes frosted over, his jaw suddenly rigid with anger. 'My company doesn't build concrete monstrosities,' he rasped.

'No?' she arched a brow mockingly.

'No,' he said tautly. 'I have some very highly qualified architects working for me, people with sensitivity.'

Her shrug was deliberately insolent. 'Only time will tell, I suppose,' she taunted.

His mouth twisted. 'Time is something I have a lot of.'

'And I thought you were a busy man,' she mocked.

'I am.' His gaze was locked challengingly with hers. 'But I can always make time for the things I want.'

She looked away from the warmth in his eyes, refusing to believe she was one of the 'things' he wanted. Let him practise his charms on the unguarded and susceptible like Bethany; she had learnt the hard way not to trust this man.

'Talking of time . . .' she stood up pointedly, 'it's getting very late.'

Jarrett made no effort to move. 'Don't let us keep you,' he taunted.

She drew in an angry breath, knowing by the way Bethany smiled her satisfaction that she would get no support from her to get Jarrett to leave. She might already be too late to talk any sense into her sister! And now that she was standing up she had no choice but to actually go to bed herself.

'I'd like to talk to you later, Bethany,' she added quietly.

'I thought it was late,' Jarrett drawled mockingly.

She shot him an angry glance. 'It's never too late to talk to my sister. Later, Bethany,' she repeated warningly.

'I'll be seeing you again soon, Sian,' Jarrett told her softly.

'Perhaps,' she nodded coolly, and left the room, her head held high.

She went through her nightly ritual of cleansing her face, taking a shower, brushing her hair until it shone, all the time conscious of the silence downstairs and the fact that she hadn't heard the sound of the powerful engine leaving.

She couldn't resist the impulse to draw back the curtain in her room; the black Porsche seemed like a predator in the glow of the street-lamp. She let the curtain fall slowly back into place, clenching her hands together. Jarrett was still downstairs with Bethany, perhaps kissing her, making love to her. When he knew she was upstairs just waiting for him to leave!

But Jarrett had never minded flaunting his attraction to other women in front of her, one woman in particular. Nina Marshall had been Jarrett's girl-friend long before Sian had known him. What she hadn't realised was that she had remained his mistress, that she would have done so even after they were married.

She could still remember the night she had discovered Jarrett's duplicity, could still feel the embarrassment and shame of the night she had found him kissing the other woman.

A stag-party, Jarrett had called it. Only Sian hadn't realised at the time that was exactly what he would behave like—a *rutting* stag!

They had decided to have their respective parties two nights before the wedding, not wanting to risk it on the eve, knowing the reputation these sort of parties had for people getting drunk. Jarrett was determined he wasn't going to have a hangover at his wedding!

And so the two of them had met their friends, in two different public houses, of course. Only her friends had decided it would be fun to join the men, and instead of them walking in on a drinking party they had found Jarrett in a corner of the room, far away from his friends, having a private party of his own—with Nina Marshall.

Sian had felt her love for him shrivel up and die when she saw the way the two of them were kissing, Jarrett's shirt unbuttoned down to his waist as Nina caressed him, the other woman's lipgloss smeared across his mouth.

She had felt the nausea rising up within her, then she had turned and run out of the bar as Jarrett surfaced long enough to call her name. And she hadn't stopped running until she reached home and the sanctuary of her bedroom.

Only it hadn't been a sanctuary for long. Jarrett had slammed in a few minutes after she had thrown herself sobbing on the bed, smelling of whisky, Nina's vivid lipgloss still on his mouth and cheek. And he had had the nerve to berate *her*, to chide her for being a fool in front of everyone over what had only been a harmless kiss.

Harmless! He and Nina had almost been making love there in front of everyone! Sian had screamed at him to get out, to stay away from her, but he hadn't stayed away, and as he came towards her she became hysterical, scratching and clawing at him until he backed off with the marks of her nails down his cheek, telling her he would talk to her in the morning when she had calmed down and decided to act like an adult and not a child.

Her father had been furious when he learnt what had happened, and had refused to let Jarrett in the house. Although that hadn't stopped him, she remembered; she had been forced to listen while he once again claimed his innocence. She had refused to believe his excuses, she already knew the truth about him and Nina. She had told him the wedding was off, that she never wanted to see him again.

Instead of marrying him the next day she had spent the time in her room, had learnt from her father that Jarrett had left Swannell that afternoon with Nina sitting beside him in the Jaguar. Sian hadn't seen Jarrett again until today.

And she wished she hadn't seen him now; she knew that he intended wreaking havoc in her life for a second time. Just by being here he was unsettling her. And he knew it, damn him!

It was half an hour later when she heard the Porsche leave, the engine a gentle purr this time, like a sleeping tiger about to pounce. Strange how the car seemed to reflect its owner's moods—first the aggression, now the patience and calm of a waiting feline.

An abashed-looking Bethany came into her room several minutes later, coming in to lean back against the dressing-table. 'I thought you might be asleep by now,' she said awkwardly.

'As you can see, I'm not.' Sian sat back against her pillows, a book open in front of her—although it was only for show, she hadn't been able to read a single word!

Her sister swallowed hard, picking up a bottle of

perfume from the dressing-table to move it about rest-lessly in her hands. 'We were—talking, and I—I forgot the time,' she explained.

'It must have been an interesting conversation,' Sian taunted.

'It was,' Bethany confirmed eagerly. 'Jarrett was telling me all about America. It sounds so exciting.'

'Really?' she said dryly.

'Yes. Look, Sian,' Bethany sighed her impatience, 'if you have something to say, then say it. Don't just keep looking at me like that!'

'Like what?'

'Accusingly!' Bethany paced the room restlessly. 'Goodness, you finished with the man years ago,' she said petulantly.

Sian's eyes narrowed. 'And you know why!'

'Because of another woman, I suppose—'

'Don't *suppose* anything, Bethany,' she snapped. 'It *was* because of another woman. I doubt Jarrett knows the meaning of the word fidelity.'

'I'm not asking for a wedding ring, for goodness' sake,' her sister scorned, her expression contrite as she saw Sian flinch. 'I'm sorry,' she sighed. 'But really, I think you're taking this dislike of Jarrett too far. I know he must have hurt you in the past for you to feel this way about him, but these things happen. At least you found out before you were married!'

'Just,' Sian acknowledged bitterly, knowing only too well the narrow escape she had had.

'And you have Chris now,' her sister pushed her point.

'Yes,' she agreed tightly. 'I just don't want to see Jarrett hurt you the way he hurt me.'

'You're too intense, Sian—I've only had one date with

him,' Bethany muttered moodily. 'And it's not as if I'm a child.'

She knew that, knew that Bethany was old enough to make her own decisions, and yet her protective instinct where her sister was concerned was too strong, too habitual to be ignored in this case. Jarrett was dangerous, and Bethany had to be made to see that.

'Jarrett mentioned that he telephoned me earlier,' she said softly.

Bethany couldn't meet her enquiring gaze. 'Yes, that's right,' she admitted distantly. 'You were out at the time.'

'Was I?'

Blue eyes flashed. 'Of course you were. You don't think I'd keep something like that from you?'

By her sister's defensive attitude she knew that was exactly what she had done, that it had indeed been Jarrett on the telephone when she returned from work this evening. Bethany always got angry when she was found out in some misdemeanour.

'So he asked you out instead?' she asked quietly.

'Yes,' Bethany snapped.

'He must have telephoned you very shortly after I'd gone out—Chris and I had barely arrived at the restaurant when you and Jarrett came in.'

'Yes—yes, he did,' her sister looked away.

'I thought you already had a date this evening?' Sian's tone was deliberately casual.

The colour flared in Bethany's cheeks before her anger took over. 'All right!' she slammed the perfume bottle back down on the dressing-table, thrusting her hands into the hip pockets of her velvet trousers. 'So I already knew it was Jarrett I was seeing when you came home,' she sighed. 'He said he wanted to talk to you, and when I told him you were with your fiancé he asked me out instead. I didn't bother to tell you when you came home because I couldn't see the point of it. You couldn't have gone out with him even if he had asked you, you're engaged to Chris.'

'Yes,' Sian nodded. 'But don't you see, he was only using you. He just wanted a woman—'

'He never touched me in that way!' her sister exclaimed indignantly.

She felt some of the tension leave her at this disclosure. At least Jarrett hadn't made love to her sister! Not yet, anyway. 'But he will, Bethany, if you continue to see him. Jarrett uses women, and when he's finished with them he throws them away,' she revealed bitterly.

'You make him sound like some sort of sex maniac,' Bethany scorned.

'He is!' Sian flushed. 'He—he needs more than one woman to satisfy his appetite. How long do you think he'll bother to even take you out when he realises you aren't going to sleep with him?'

A reckless light entered her sister's deep blue eyes. 'Who says I'm not?' she asked defiantly.

Sian had handled this badly, she could see that by the way Bethany was behaving. 'Bethany—'

'I've already agreed to see him tomorrow, Sian,' her sister told her stubbornly. 'And I have no intention of cancelling my date with him.'

She sighed. 'Nothing I can say will change your mind?'

'Nothing!'

'Then there's nothing more to be said. Although I doubt Dad was pleased to see Jarrett here tonight . . . ?' Sian quirked questioning brows.

Again Bethany blushed. 'I—I met Jarrett in town. I wanted to see Jane about something,' she named her friend, 'and I thought it stupid for him to come all the way out here when I was going to be in town anyway. I met him at his hotel.'

Sian could just imagine what the gossips had made of that! It had been the Swan where Jarrett had held his stag party three years ago, and Fred and Ida Barlowe were still the proprietors. The locals had probably had a field-day gossiping about the fact that her sister was calling for Jarrett there.

'Dad will find out, you know that, don't you?' she prompted gently.

Bethany's mouth set rebelliously. 'I can't understand what all the fuss is about. You were going to marry Jarrett years ago, but you didn't, and you seem relieved that you didn't, so what does it matter that I'm going out with him?'

'I just don't want you hurt—'

'I'm not going to be,' her sister sighed her impatience. 'I like being with him, he's different—and exciting. But I'll probably settle down quite happily in a couple of years' time with one of the local men.'

'You don't know how deeply Jarrett can inflict pain—'

'But you obviously do.' Bethany's eyes were narrowed questioningly. 'Do you still care for him yourself, Sian, is that what's wrong?'

'No!' Sian's mouth was tight. 'I can see that nothing I do or say is going to change your mind about him, so I'll just have to let you find out for yourself. Just remember this conversation—'

'I don't need any "I told you so's"!' her sister flashed.

'You aren't getting any,' Sian said wearily, putting her book down on the bedside table. 'I just want you to remember I was concerned for you.'

'You always are,' Bethany said crossly as she went to

the door, taking the broad hint to leave. 'But I'm nineteen, Sian, old enough to make my own mistakes.'

'I'm glad you can see Jarrett is one!'

'Oh, you're impossible!' Bethany snapped. 'I like him, and I find him exciting to be with. I shall continue to see him for as long as he wants me to!'

Sian stared up at the ceiling once her sister had gone to her own room, thinking once again how badly she had handled the conversation. But she was too close to it, that was the trouble, she couldn't think or talk about Jarrett rationally.

Exciting, Bethany called him, and she had to acknowledge that Jarrett had an appeal that had in no way lessened through the years, in fact his obvious wealth seemed to have increased his arrogant assurance, and so heightened that air of authority and command that had always been a fundamental part of him. He was the sort of man who would easily impress someone as unworldly as Bethany, might even have affected Sian in the same way if she hadn't already been burnt rather badly by his cruelty.

Her father didn't seem aware of the tension between Bethany and herself the next morning, reading the morning newspaper with his usual thoroughness as he ate a leisurely breakfast, before making his usual cheerful goodbye to them both.

But Sian knew it could only be a matter of time before her father found out Bethany was seeing Jarrett. And he wouldn't be pleased. He had sworn when Jarrett hurt her so badly that the other man would never enter his house again. He would be furious when he learnt that he already had!

'I'm not going to apologise for last night,' Bethany

spoke stubbornly from the doorway, ready to leave for work herself.

Sian looked up from the washing-up. 'I didn't think you were,' she shrugged.

'And I'm not going to change my mind about seeing Jarrett tonight either.'

'No.'

Bethany sighed her frustration with this sudden calm. 'Why don't you scream and shout?' she scowled. 'Tell me I'm a bitch for seeing him at all.'

Sian's mouth quirked with wry humour. 'But I don't think you are a bitch, you're just another of Jarrett's victims.'

'You make him sound lethal!'

'He is.'

'Oh, Sian, that's so melodramatic,' Bethany dismissed impatiently. 'He's just a man.'

'Yes,' Sian agreed bitterly. 'Except that he plays the game of love by rules no one else is familiar with.'

'I'm not in love with him!' her sister sighed.

'Not yet.' She turned away.

'Would it bother you if I were?' Bethany asked quietly.

'You would only end up getting hurt,' Sian didn't directly answer the question.

Bethany shrugged. 'I'll face that, if it ever happens. I have to go now. I'll see you lunchtime?'

'Of course,' she confirmed dryly. 'Where else would I be but here?'

'I'll cook lunch, if you like,' Bethany offered generously.

'If you're sure we're all up to it,' she teased; all of them were familiar with the fact that cooking was not Bethany's biggest talent.

Her sister grimaced. 'I don't think even I could ruin a salad.'

'No?' Sian mocked softly. 'I seem to remember that you burnt the new potatoes the last time you prepared us a salad.'

Bethany smiled as the tension between them eased a little. 'I'll leave the potatoes for you to do when you get in.'

'Okay,' laughed Sian. 'Have a good morning.'

Instead of leaving Bethany ran across the room to hug Sian, her youthful face pleading. 'I'm sorry I'm such a nuisance to you,' she smiled tremulously. 'I really don't mean to hurt you.'

Sian smiled back at her. 'I know that, love,' she said huskily.

'I—I have to see Jarrett. You understand that, don't you?' she cajoled pleadingly.

She understood only too well her sister's driving need to see Jarrett, had once been consumed by that need herself. But she wouldn't let Jarrett hurt her sister as he had hurt her! If Bethany couldn't be made to see sense then Jarrett would have to be the one she talked to. And soon.

'I understand,' she nodded.

'Thank you!' Bethany hugged her again before leaving.

Yes, she understood. Oh, how she understood! Jarrett couldn't do this, he just couldn't!

But he would, she knew he would. And he hadn't been averse to evoking some painful memories for her last night, reminding her all too vividly of the way he had made love to her. Jarrett had made love with an unequalled eroticism, had claimed at the time that she *did* equal it.

She determinedly put these soul-destroying thoughts from her mind, knew that to think of Jarrett as he had once seemed to her *would* surely destroy her.

''Morning.' Ginny was sitting at Sian's desk when she arrived at the surgery. 'I hope you're in a better mood than Chris,' she grimaced. 'He's in a foul temper.'

Sian had no intention of telling Ginny the reason for her brother's bad mood, although she could see that was what the other girl was waiting for. 'I'm fine,' she smiled blandly.

Ginny looked disappointed by this answer. 'You don't happen to know what's upset my big brother, do you?' She stood up.

Sian took her place at the desk and began to deal with the post. 'I have no idea. Why don't you ask him?'

'Because he'll probably tell me to mind my own business!' She sighed at Sian's pointed look. 'All right, so maybe I should. But there isn't much that upsets Chris, and the last two days his temper has defied description.'

Yes, it had, now that she thought about it. Could Chris possibly have known of Jarrett's return before last night? His father was a member of the local Council, maybe he had mentioned Jarrett's possible return to his son. It was a strong possibility, the two men were very close. Poor Chris, it must have been hard to keep the confidence to himself, especially knowing of her past relationship with the man as he did. He must have been very worried. He still appeared to be, which was silly after the way she had reassured him last night.

He didn't exactly seem in a bad temper when she saw him later that morning, more preoccupied, and the work load was very heavy, not allowing time for conversation.

'Why didn't you tell me?' Ginny accused with eagerness as Sian pulled on her jacket in preparation for leaving for lunch.

She looked up, her hazel eyes puzzled. 'Tell you what?'

Ginny looked scandalised by her lack of comprehension. 'About meeting Jarrett King last night.'

'Oh, that.' Sian looked away.

'Oh, that!' the other girl echoed impatiently. 'Chris is all bitter and twisted about it, and you dismiss it as if it were nothing!'

'It was nothing,' Sian insisted coolly. 'And I'm sure you've misunderstood Chris's reaction—he understood perfectly about Jarrett.'

'One of the pet owners mentioned to him that he'd seen the three of you talking last night, and Chris was very cutting. He's jealous,' Ginny said incredulously.

'He has no need to be.'

'Doesn't he?' Ginny gave her a strange look.

'No,' Sian sighed her impatience.

Ginny's dark brows rose. 'Then why is Jarrett King here?' she asked softly. 'I doubt he's come to ask Chris for his professional opinion about anything,' she added derisively.

Sian turned with a start as the bell rang over the door as it opened, looking straight into amused green eyes. Jarrett seemed enormous in the small reception area.

'Ladies,' he drawled in greeting, the green of his shirt a perfect match for his emerald eyes, the cream trousers moulded against the lean length of his legs.

'Mr King,' Ginny greeted enthusiastically.

Jarrett looked coolly at Sian, forcing her to make the introductions, if resentfully.

'I'm Chris's sister,' Ginny added with a grin. 'And he isn't at all pleased by your return to Swannell.'

'Indeed?' Jarrett seemed amused, his husky voice charming the other woman.

'But we don't all feel that way,' Ginny continued eagerly.

'Thank you.' Jarrett's slow warm smile was designed to attract her—and it succeeded, much to Sian's disgust. 'I've come to steal Sian away for a few hours,' he added softly.

'Go ahead,' Ginny nodded. 'She was just leaving anyway.'

'Sian?' he quirked dark blond brows at her.

Aware of Ginny's avid interest, she nodded distantly. 'I can spare you a few minutes.'

'I was thinking more in the direction of lunch.' He opened the door for her to exit.

'I don't think so,' she refused once they were out of the surgery and standing on the busy pavement.

Jarrett's eyes narrowed to green slits, power emanating from his lean body. 'Why not?' he probed softly.

'In case you've forgotten,' a false smile curved her lips, knowing that Jarrett never forgot anything. She was conscious of the curious stares they were attracting; this was a small town, and most of the people rushing by them were acquainted with one or both of them. 'I'm engaged to be married.'

'Does that mean you don't have to eat?' he taunted.

'I always have my lunch at home.'

'Always?'

'Yes!' she snapped.

'In that case, perhaps I could save you the walk and drive you home?' he offered smoothly.

'I—Yes, okay,' she accepted, seeing his face sharpen with suspicion. And well it might! She intended taking this opportunity to talk to him about Bethany. 'Thank you,' she nodded distantly.

He opened the passenger door to the Porsche; the powerful car was blatantly parked in a no-parking area. Sian climbed inside, finding the intimacy of the interior quite overwhelming once he had got in beside her.

Jarrett drove the car without effort, turning to smile at her. 'We would have been eating in a public restaurant, you know, not my hotel room.'

'I'm aware of that.' She refused to even look at him.

'Half the problem, hmm?' he taunted throatily. 'You never used to mind being seen in public with me,' he added harshly.

Her gaze remained fixedly ahead. 'That was a long time ago, and I—Where are you going?' she gasped as he missed the turning to her home.

'Never give me an advantage of any kind, Sian,' he told her grimly, his hair gleaming golden in the summer sunshine.

'A-advantage?'

'By getting in the car you gave me control over our destination. If I had my way I would drive away from here and never turn back. Oh, don't worry,' he mocked her shocked expression, 'I'm not going to do that. I want you willingly—or not at all.'

Sian had gone very white, no longer able to contain even a vestige of the icy control she had been treating him with, her eyes wide with panic.

Jarrett was slowing the Porsche down now, turning down the road that went towards the river. 'Don't look like that, Sian,' he chided gently. 'It can be no surprise to you why I'm here in Swannell.'

'I—The hotel and shopping centre . . .' she swallowed

convulsively, terrified of the familiar warmth of desire in his eyes.

'Damn the hotel and shopping centre,' he dismissed arrogantly. 'I came back for you, Sian. Only for you.'

CHAPTER FOUR

'I STILL want you, Sian.'

As soon as Jarrett had stopped the car she had got out, moving as far away from him as possible and standing at the river's edge.

She had believed she had imagined Jarrett's words in the car, that he couldn't possibly have come back to Swannell to see her. But the savage intensity in his face as she turned to look at him now made her recoil in fear. 'No!' she cried as his hands came out towards her. 'Don't touch me!' she cringed.

He drew in a harsh breath, his hands dropping slowly to his sides. 'Don't look at me like that!' he rasped, his eyes bleak.

'Then don't say these things to me!' She moved jerkily away from him to walk along the embankment, stopping as she saw where her legs had unwittingly taken her. She came to an abrupt halt, staring in numbed fascination at the huge willow tree, its weeping branches giving refuge beneath their coolness.

She couldn't move as Jarrett stepped close into the back of her, his hands coming to rest possessively on her hips as he pulled her close to him, his face buried in the red sheen of her hair as he breathed warmly against her temple. 'Our place, Sian,' he said throatily. 'Come with me there now, darling.' He moved to stand in front of her. 'Come with me and—'

'No!' She stepped away from him, her eyes wide and shocked. 'How dare you talk to me like that?'

His eyes blazed down at her, his face contorted with fury. 'I dare because I have no intention of letting you marry Christopher Newman!'

'*You* have no intention?' she scorned shrilly, her body stiff with outrage. 'After three years you think your wants and needs *matter* to me?'

'They'd damn well better,' he ground out. 'I can't let you marry him, Sian,' his voice lowered persuasively. 'It would kill me to see you married to another man.'

'You should have thought of that before,' she choked, seeing the fire burning in his eyes, knowing he meant every word. 'Before you chose Nina Marshall over me.'

His face darkened. 'How many times do I have to tell you she meant nothing to me?'

'You don't,' she said wearily. 'Just leave me alone now. I marry Chris in a month's time, so just stay away from me.'

'I can't. And you know damn well I can't!'

'You have done all this time—'

'Because it was what you wanted—'

'It's what I still want!' she told him heatedly.

'You belong to me!' Jarrett bit out fiercely.

'I'm marrying Chris!'

He slowly shook his head. 'You gave yourself to me beneath that willow tree, Sian. And you'll stay mine! I told you, I came back for you. I've had the *Swannell Chronicle*,' he named the local newspaper, 'sent to me ever since I left. I saw the announcement of your engagement three months ago, just before my uncle died, and I got here as soon as I could.'

'You honestly expect me to believe that the announcement of my engagement to Chris was enough to make you leave New York and come here?' she derided.

'I didn't just leave, Sian,' he told her grimly. 'If it had

just been me I would have been here months ago. But I'm transferring the whole company over here. No easy feat, believe me. That's the reason I was almost too late to stop this wedding, the arrangements to transfer the company took longer than I expected.'

'You *are* too late,' she said firmly. 'The moment I found out about you and Nina it was too late. Three years is too long to wait to come back and apologise.' Her sarcasm was barely concealed.

Jarrett's mouth tightened. 'I have nothing to apologise for.'

'Nina—'

'God, when will you believe that what you saw was just a last evening of fun—'

'Oh, you consider marriage to me would have stopped all your fun?' she said harshly.

'No, I don't mean that at all,' he sighed his impatience with her. 'Stop twisting things to fit in with what you want to believe,' he snapped.

'I *saw* you, Jarrett.'

'You saw one kiss, damn it! *One kiss*,' he repeated heatedly. 'On a stag night.'

She turned away. 'It was the kisses I didn't see that bothered me the most,' she bit out tightly.

'There were none!'

'No?' she said bitterly, knowing that he lied to her.

'No! Oh, to hell with this,' he dismissed disgustedly, coming determinedly towards her. 'I can't reach you with words.'

Sian saw the fiery intent in his eyes, and she backed away from it. Jarrett let her go, slowly advancing, and suddenly she knew why, as the branches of the willow brushed against her face. 'No . . . !' she cried as she realised his intention.

'Yes,' he groaned, pushing her remorselessly beneath the willow's sheltering branches, a world strangely apart, tiny shafts of sunlight penetrating the gloom as the branches moved gently in the breeze. 'God, *yes*, Sian!' His body was suddenly hard against hers as he gathered her into his arms, just holding her lightly for several minutes, neither of them speaking, their hearts beating in a tattoo of unison. 'Feel how my body responds to you,' he moaned as his thighs surged into hers. 'Only you have ever had this instantaneous effect on me.'

'Me, and every other woman you've slept with!' Her voice came out as a whisper, it somehow seemed like sacrilege to break the enchanting peace beneath the willow with harsh, loud words.

'Only ever you, Sian.' He was kissing her throat now, all the way to where the vee of her brown blouse met over her breasts. 'All the others had to work at it. With you I've only ever had to look at you.'

'How embarrassing for you!' She tried to hold on to her sanity as she felt him begin to unbutton her blouse and slip it off her shoulder, his warm probing lips tasting every inch of the flesh he exposed.

'It can be, at times,' his voice rumbled low in his chest.

'And how many "others" have there been while you were in America?' she taunted to hide the rapidly rising heat of her body, the wildfire excitement she had thought never to know again.

'None,' he rasped abruptly. 'And you never did tell me if Newman is your lover.' He was looking down at her now, a curious stillness surrounding them as he waited for her answer. 'Sian!' he finally prompted in an agonised voice.

She couldn't believe him about the women in America, she knew his demanding sensuality too well to imagine him going without a woman for three *days*, let alone three years! 'He isn't,' she told him calmly. 'But—'

'*God*, Sian!' he shuddered against her as his arms tightened convulsively.

'But I enjoy his lovemaking,' she finished in a tight voice, gasping as Jarrett crushed her to him, feeling as if her ribs would break from the pressure. 'Jarrett, you're hurting me!' she groaned, feeling faint with pain.

The tension about her ribs at once lessened, although his breathing was still harsh. 'As you are deliberately hurting me! Whatever he does to you it isn't making love. I've already explained to you that—'

'Only you can make love to me,' she mocked. 'You overestimate yourself, Jarrett.'

'And you didn't learn anything from the car journey just now,' his mouth was twisted, the glitter of his eyes discernible as she became accustomed to the darkness. 'I warned you not to give me any advantage, Sian,' he taunted, 'or I would take it. Being here, alone with me like this, is more than an advantage, it's a gift!' His teeth gleamed whitely as he smiled.

It *was* dangerous, she realised that now. Her position was precarious; Jarrett's strength, as she knew from experience, was ten times more than hers—a fact he took advantage of as he unbalanced her enough to send her falling softly on to the ground, quickly following her, the lean length of his body pinning her to the mossy floor.

'I've dreamt about this, Sian,' he spoke against the parted moistness of her mouth. 'Fantasised about it. Every night for three years I've dreamt of holding you in my arms again,' he groaned, 'longed to find release in your body, to—'

'No more, Jarrett!' she moaned in a pained voice,

knowing she could no more stand his seduction with words than she could the intimacy of his body moving against hers.

'No, no more words,' he agreed throatily. 'Let's just *feel*, Sian. Touch me, darling, the way you used to. And once I've made love to you again you'll be mine.'

Being with him like this beneath the willow brought back the memory of too many shared intimacies for her to fight what she really wanted to do, and her caresses were as sure and pleasure-giving as his were as she smoothed the shirt from the steely strength of his shoulders, sighing her satisfaction as she felt each muscle and sinew react to her touch.

As his mouth met with hers she felt as if she had come home after a long journey, knew that the heated gentleness of his lips devouring hers wiped out the last three years as if they had only been minutes, everyone and everything forgotten as she once again knew the sureness of his hands loving her body. Her breasts flowered beneath his hands, the nipples hard and sensitive to his every touch, pleasure shuddering through her body as his mouth suckled the throbbing swell before it moved slowly down, down . . .

He removed her clothes with slow thoroughness, gazing down at the silky cream of her flesh in the flickering sunlight. 'You've matured, Sian,' he spoke throatily. 'Your body has smoothed out, your breasts are larger, and your thighs . . . ! God, you're even more beautiful, Sian,' he kissed her stomach with slow loving care, moving down to the silkiness of her thighs, finding the centre of her passion as he eased the ache to a burst of fire, allowing her no respite from his practised caresses until she shuddered beneath him in a spasm of uncontrollable sensation that left her weak and gasping.

'Oh, Sian,' he groaned. 'Nothing between us has changed. Nothing!' He quickly removed the rest of his clothes, his body covering hers as their thighs met, making Sian long for the rhythm of passion to explode between them, to be joined with him, to leave them spiralling down the tunnel of ecstatic spasms that all lovers share as they know that moment of exquisite death before the mindless pleasure, as wave after wave of burning desire ripped through the body.

Jarrett was heavy above her, his breath coming in short strangled gasps as he waited for her to be completely ready for him, weak with the same longing. 'Three years,' he murmured wonderingly. 'Three long lonely years, when I was sure my memories of being with you like this must have become exaggerated in my mind. Instead it's more, so much more. Oh, let me love you, Sian, let me love you completely!'

Sian heard what he was saying, and it all came back to her, all the pain, the disillusionment of loving a man like this. She couldn't go through it again!

Jarrett tasted the tears on her cheeks as his lips slowly caressed her face, and he raised his head with a frown. 'Tears . . . ?' His tone was puzzled. 'Darling—'

'Get away from me,' she ordered in a cold voice, her eyes dull with pain, knowing this had to stop—now!

'Sian—'

She pushed him away and pulled on her clothes, her face averted as she felt him search the rigid coldness of her expression. Her mouth twisted in self-disgust.

Jarrett drew in a ragged breath, pale and dazed by the scorching passion they had just shared, the hand he held out to her falling unheeded to his side. 'Sian, I love you,' he told her in a voice choked with emotion.

Her head snapped round in fury. 'You don't know the

meaning of the word! If you did you would never have—have tried to make love to me,' she swallowed convulsively, burying her face in her hands as she cried softly.

Jarrett moved away from her, pulling on his own discarded clothing with decisive movements. 'I wanted to make love to you, Sian,' he rasped coldly. 'And you were enjoying it.'

'*Yes*, damn you!' she choked, glaring at him. 'I came with you to talk about Bethany, instead I—I almost let you make love to me.'

'Bethany?' His expression sharpened. He was fully dressed now, only the flush to his lean cheeks and the untidy blondness of his hair betraying the fact that he was still deeply disturbed by their lovemaking. 'What does she have to do with us?'

Sian smoothed her skirt over her thighs, her hands shaking slightly, her body still pulsating from the first complete passion she had known since Jarrett had gone away. She was full of self-disgust at what she had done, full of self-recriminations, of confusion. God, what was she going to do? Jarrett had destroyed all her pride in herself, had shown her all too easily how susceptible she was to the instincts of her body, the dictates of her brain not meaning a thing when Jarrett so much as touched her.

What today would mean to her relationship with Chris, with her marriage to him, she had yet to think. She *daren't* think; she knew that she had betrayed Chris and their engagement by what she had almost done today.

Her gaze was bitter as she looked at Jarrett, physically hating him in that moment. He had known exactly what he was doing just now, he had set out to make love to her. Not that he had received much of a fight! She was deeply ashamed of the easy conquest she had made.

'There is no us,' she told him abruptly. 'And I want you to stop seeing Bethany.'

His eyes narrowed, his expression taut with anger, the lover of a few minutes ago completely gone now. 'Why?' he rasped.

'Because you'll only hurt her—'

'She's a big girl now,' he shrugged.

'She's nineteen,' Sian said fiercely. 'And she can't see you for what you are.'

Jarrett stiffened at her insulting tone. 'What am I?' he ground out slowly, as if he knew in advance that he wasn't going to like the answer.

She drew in a ragged breath. 'A selfish bastard who takes what he wants, when he wants, regardless of anyone else's feelings. And I don't mean mine,' she added at his derisive snort.

'You didn't seem to be giving your fiancé much thought just now either!'

Sian paled, suddenly feeling sick. 'I know that. And I'm not proud of it.'

'Sian, I told you, I *love* you.' Jarrett took a step towards her, his expression softening. 'You have no need to feel ashamed of what just happened. We were always explosive together. And we will be in future.'

'I'm marrying Chris!' she said with more conviction than truth, not sure what she was doing now, not when she still had this weakness towards Jarrett.

'Like hell you are!' he returned through clenched teeth. 'God, Sian, he'll be hurt at first, any man would be if he lost you, but as you haven't been lovers he won't find it as painful as I did.'

'Painful!' she scorned. 'You had Nina to salve your— pain.'

'I didn't want Nina, I wanted you. I still do. You belonged to me then, Sian, and you still belong to me. We just proved that,' he added softly. 'I won't let you throw yourself away on Chris Newman!'

'You won't stop me!'

'No?' he taunted grimly. 'And if I refuse to stop seeing Bethany until you come to me?'

Her eyes widened with disbelief. 'You wouldn't do that?' she gasped.

'I would,' he nodded curtly. 'And Bethany is far from averse to my making love to her.'

'Jarrett—'

'My life depends on this, Sian. Until you come to me I shall continue to see Bethany. It would be a pity to have to seduce your sister in an effort to bring you to your senses.' He looked at her challengingly.

'That would just make me hate you more!' she spat out.

'I'd rather have your hate than nothing,' he rasped.

'Then you have it!' She turned to leave the seclusion beneath the willow, stopping as she heard the sound of a dog barking nearby, a man's voice calling to it as he too drew close. 'God,' she groaned in a whisper. 'We could be seen,' she frowned her consternation.

Jarrett scowled at her hunted look. 'I'm not concerned—'

'But I am. *I am!*' She gave him a wild-eyed look. 'I had to live in this town once before when you made a fool of me. I won't be a subject for ridicule at your expense again. I have to get out of here, and if you care anything for me at all you'll let me walk far away before you leave too.'

'You can leave, Sian.' He was suddenly close once again. 'And I won't attempt to follow until you're safely away from here. But I meant what I said,' his warm breath ruffled the hair at her nape as he stood behind her. 'Until you come to me of your own free will, to *stay* with me, then I'll continue to see Bethany. And make it soon, Sian, or I won't be responsible for the consequences.'

She swallowed hard. 'Bethany . . . ?'

'Yes,' his expression was harsh.

She breathed raggedly. 'You never did play fair, Jarrett.'

'I never played at all,' he derided softly. 'About you I've always been completely serious. I should have come back sooner, should never have let you drift into this engagement with Newman.' He shook his head. 'I left here in a temper, intending to come back for you when you'd had time to come to your senses. But—things weren't as straightforward in the States as they at first appeared. My uncle needed me, and you were so young I thought I had time.' His mouth twisted bitterly. 'I had no time at all.'

'Three years,' she reminded him harshly. 'Three long years.'

'You think they weren't long for me too? God, they were more than long, they were agonising! But you were too much of a child then, Sian, and your love and trust died at the first hurdle. I wanted a woman for my wife, not a distrustful child who wouldn't believe a word I said. My uncle was ill, he needed me, and the business filled most of my time. Except the night,' he added bleakly. 'At night I couldn't banish the tormenting thoughts of making love to you. I won't let you go out of my life again, Sian, so you might as well accept that.'

The dog's barking had faded into the distance now. 'I'm leaving now,' she told him stiltedly. 'If you choose to see Bethany, that's between you and her.'

'And you won't mind, hmm?'

'No!' she said determinedly.

'You'll mind, Sian,' he warned softly. 'It will eat you up alive, slowly but surely. And when you're crying out for mercy I'll be waiting.'

With one last strangled cry Sian pushed the branches of the willow aside, running for all she was worth, although knowing that Jarrett didn't follow her. Why should he? He was playing a waiting game, sure by her impassioned response to him just now that it was only a matter of time. And wasn't it? Dear God, wasn't it!

Her heart had leapt when he told her he loved her, and her senses still swam from his fierce lovemaking, her whole body filled with an ache she hadn't know for three years, an ache that longed to be assuaged.

Could she believe that he had always meant to come back for her? Did she *want* to believe it? And if she did, what future could there ever be for them? Jarrett had let her down once only days before their wedding, had later callously rejected the woman he left her for. Who was to say that he wouldn't again tire of her and turn to another woman?

And what of her engagement to Chris? He was a good man, he deserved more loyalty than she had shown him today. Heavens, she couldn't believe the easy way she had fallen into Jarrett's arms. Within twenty-four hours of his return to Swannell she had been making love with him!

So what did that make her love for Chris? She couldn't possibly still be in love with Jarrett—every thought she had told her that. It was just physical attraction she felt for him, nothing more. But it was enough to make her forget every principle she had ever been taught, all decency, to make her the pliant lover he wanted, to making her a victim of her own desire.

She hurried home, wanting to hide away from the world, sure that anyone who looked at her would know what she had almost done. It was bad enough that she should know of it, if anyone else should even guess—!

Bethany was just on her way back to work when Sian arrived home, pausing in the act of getting into her car. 'Hey, what happened to you at lunchtime? I—Sian?' her voice sharpened with concern. 'Are you feeling all right?'

Sian summoned up a tight smile, knowing how dishevelled she must look. 'I'm fine. It was just a busy morning, I got delayed. Did you manage lunch okay?'

Her sister grinned. 'I burnt the potatoes again, but not as badly this time.'

Sian's mouth twisted wryly. 'I'm sure Dad was grateful for that.'

'He didn't say much,' her sister chuckled. 'He's gone back to work, by the way. I left your lunch in the fridge.'

The thought of food turned her stomach over. 'Thanks,' she said abruptly, thinking how young and carefree her sister looked. Had she ever felt that free? She couldn't remember it if she had.

'Are you sure you're all right?' Bethany frowned. 'You seem a little—strange. Not yourself.'

After what she had just shared with Jarrett Sian wasn't sure she wanted to be herself. She would much rather be someone else, someone who couldn't make love with one man and marry another.

'I have a headache,' she invented—although the

words seemed to conjure one up, a painful throbbing was starting in her temples. 'You had better get back to work.' Her smile was strained.

'Mm.' Bethany slid in behind the wheel of the car, talking out of the opened window. 'Take some aspirin and lie down for a while. You really don't look well.'

She raised a hand in parting as Bethany reversed the car out of the driveway, the pounding in her head now making her wince.

She didn't want to think any more, wanted to find oblivion in sleep. She took two aspirins before lying down on her bed, keeping her mind deliberately blank. And yet sleep evaded her, the ache in her body for the deep satisfaction only Jarrett had ever given her making it impossible to do more than lie awake in an agony of longing.

She was pale but composed at evening surgery; she had managed to convince herself that her time with Jarrett that afternoon had just been a horrendous nightmare, that she couldn't possibly have behaved so wantonly.

It was a busy surgery, and she was glad of the diversion, once more putting off the reality of the enormity of what she had done, hiding behind polite smiles and cool efficiency.

It was almost the end of surgery when the telephone on her desk rang for about the tenth time that evening, the last cat having gone through to be examined by Chris. She hoped this wasn't a call that would take Chris out on an emergency; he was the vet on call today. She wanted to be with him tonight, sure that once she was with him, secure in his love, Jarrett would fade into the background once more.

'Sian?'

She stiffened as she recognised his voice. 'Yes?' Her tone was cold.

Jarrett chuckled, his voice warm and velvety when he spoke again. 'I just wanted to talk to you, Sian.'

'What about?' she snapped, aware that Mrs Granger and her black tomcat were leaving now, and giving the other woman a vague smile as she went out the door.

'You know damn well what, Sian,' the laughter could be heard in his tone. 'Although I'd rather be waking up in your arms than talking. Do you remember the way we always slept in each other's arms after we'd made love?' he mused. 'I missed that today. But next time we won't stop—'

She slowly replaced the receiver, staring at it as if it were a viper about to strike her. When the telephone began ringing again she continued to stare at it, in no doubt as to who the caller was.

One of the inner doors opened and Martin put his head round the door, frowning as he saw Sian's wide-eyed stare. 'Aren't you going to answer that?' he asked slowly, his dark good looks boyishly attractive.

She could feel a nerve beating erratically in her cheek, a nervous twitch she had no control over. 'Of course.' She moistened her lips as she once again picked up the receiver.

'Could the vet come at once?' a woman's panicked voice asked. 'My dog has been hit by a car and—'

'It's an injured dog.' Sian put her hand over the mouthpiece to tell Martin.

'Put it straight through to Chris,' he advised softly.

She did so, sensing Martin's puzzled gaze still on her as she put her receiver down, turning to smile at him. 'I was miles away,' she explained.

He grinned. 'Thinking of the wedding?'

She was sure she paled even more, although the smile remained fixed to her lips. 'Yes,' she lied.

'Not long to go now, hmm?'

'No.' Her voice was husky. She had been sure that second call was Jarrett telephoning back. It was just like him to unnerve her by *not* calling back. Damn him!

'Are you sure you're all right?' Martin watched the play of emotions across her face.

'I just have a headache.' The throb in her temples had stayed with her; Jarrett's call, the implications behind it, had not helped at all.

'Do you, darling?' Chris sounded preoccupied as he came out of his surgery. 'Take some Paracetemol,' he advised absently, pulling on his jacket in preparation for leaving.

'I—'

'I have to go, Sian.' He kissed her lightly on the mouth. 'Mrs Jacobs' dog has been hurt. But I should be back in time to go to Mr Small's.'

'Mr Small's? But—' Oh dear, they had to see the vicar tonight about choosing the hymns for their wedding! She had forgotten all about that in the chaos of Jarrett's return. 'Oh yes,' she realised dully. 'Well, don't worry, Chris,' she said brightly. 'I'm sure we can cancel and go another night if you don't make it.'

He nodded. 'If I'm not there by eight-fifteen call him and explain. I have to go.' He hurried out of the door.

Sian looked up to see the indecision on Martin's face, and guessed the reason for it. 'Don't look like that,' she teased. 'You have tonight off, remember?'

'Yes. But if you have to see the vicar . . .'

'We can do it another night.' She stood up decisively. 'It's only a question of telling Mr Small which hymns we want played.'

'And listen to his pep-talk,' Martin grinned, his blue eyes gleaming with mischief.

Sian frowned. 'What pep-talk?'

'The one about sex, although important, being only part of marriage. It's a damned nice part, though,' he added with relish.

'I'll tell Ginny you said so,' she answered him vaguely. She had forgotten about these little talks the vicar liked to have with couples getting married; she had already been through it once with Jarrett, the difference being that *they* had already known of the importance of a good sexual relationship.

'She already knows,' Martin chuckled. 'I'll lock up here if you want to get home,' he offered.

'I'm in no hurry—'

'Oh, go on,' he encouraged. 'I'm feeling generous.'

Sian didn't argue with him any further, but collected her jacket and left. It had been a long day, a traumatic one, and her nerves were decidedly frayed. She hoped Chris didn't get back in time tonight, she would rather give the vicar a miss for now. The last thing she needed was a lecture on the sanctity of marriage, when she had almost broken one of the Ten Commandments today, morally at least. She wore Chris's ring, that meant she already belonged to him, and she had only just drawn back from Jarrett's possession of her.

Her father was alone in the lounge when she arrived home, and she knew instantly, by his wary expression, that he knew Jarrett was back. She avoided his gaze. 'Like a cup of tea?'

He stood up. 'I'll make you one,' he offered. 'Like anything to eat?'

'No, thanks.' She sat down with a weary sigh, resting her head back against the sofa.

'Busy day?' Her father paused in the doorway.

'Not really,' she gave a wan smile. 'Just a long one.'

'I'll get the tea,' he nodded.

Sian was glad of this time alone to collect her thoughts together, knowing that her father was going to talk about Jarrett. The whole town seemed to be talking about Jarrett!

'There you go, love.' Her father handed her a steaming cup of tea minutes later.

She took a huge swallow, grimacing as she tasted sugar. 'Dad!' she pulled a face.

'I thought you needed the glucose.' He looked down at her with concerned blue eyes.

She still avoided his gaze. 'No Bethany tonight?'

He shrugged and sat down opposite her. 'She's gone out for the evening,' he said huskily.

'Really. Who—' she broke off, suddenly knowing why Jarrett hadn't called her back earlier. He would have been late for his date with Bethany if he had! 'That's nice,' she gave a tight smile.

Her father sighed. 'It isn't nice at all,' he scowled. 'The man's already hurt one of my daughters, he has no right to come back and hurt the other one.'

Sian swallowed hard. 'You mean Jarrett?'

'Who else?' Her father stood up to pace the room, his hands thrust into his pockets as he hunched over. 'You knew Bethany was seeing him?' he frowned down at her.

'Yes,' she nodded.

'And you didn't tell me?'

'What could I say, Dad?' she pleaded. 'Bethany is an adult, of age, she can see who she wants.'

'But Jarrett King!'

'Yes,' she sighed dully.

His expression softened. 'I'm sorry, pet. You must feel awful about it.'

Awful? She refused to even think how she felt about Jarrett seeing her sister. 'It was a long time ago, Dad,' she said evasively. 'I'm engaged to Chris now.'

'Yes, thank God,' he sighed. 'Jarrett's even more arrogant than before—'

'You met him?' she gasped her surprise.

'He called for Bethany here,' he explained grimly. 'The man has the cheek of the devil. In fact, they're probably related!'

Sian's mouth curved into a rueful smile. 'Probably,' she nodded.

'Jarrett's got nerve enough to have come after you if you hadn't already been engaged to Chris.' He watched as the delicate colour flooded her cheeks, and frowned deeply. 'He's stayed away from you, hasn't he?'

'Of course, Dad—'

'Sian?' he questioned suspiciously.

She stood up, her tea finished, putting the cup to one side. 'He knows I'm engaged, Dad.'

'That doesn't answer my question,' he said slowly.

'I can't answer it, Dad,' she sighed. 'I've spoken to Jarrett, that much must be obvious. It's also obvious that he's seeing Bethany.'

'Do you mind?'

The colour ebbed from her face as rapidly as it had entered. 'I have no right to mind. I have to go and change, Dad,' she added firmly. 'Chris will be here soon.'

'I wish the man had never come back,' her father mumbled. 'He was always trouble, I have no reason to suppose he'll be any different this time.'

'He has business here, Dad,' she reasoned.

'Mm,' he looked sceptical. 'So Bethany told me. I just hope he concludes his business quickly and leaves.'

'I'm sure he will,' she soothed. 'After all, Swannell wasn't big enough to hold him before. Now that he knows the sophistication of New York it must hold even less appeal. Don't worry, Dad, I'm sure he'll be gone soon.'

'I hope so.'

Sian mentally echoed those sentiments as she changed for her date with Chris. Maybe when Jarrett had gone she could settle down to a life of normality once again. Maybe . . .

Chris arrived back in plenty of time to go and see the vicar; the dog he had been called out to attend was not as badly injured as had been implied. Sian felt her betrayal of this trusting man even more strongly as she listened to the vicar talk to them, the pitfalls of marriage seeming to apply to her even before she was married.

But she wanted to be a good wife to Chris, wanted to forget about Jarrett. She deeply regretted her lapse of this afternoon. Lapse? It had been a landslide!

'You're very preoccupied tonight, darling,' Chris frowned as they drove back to her home.

'Just tired,' she dismissed lightly.

'It isn't my bad temper of this morning, is it?' he queried ruefully. 'I was thinking of Jarrett King last night, and—well, I suppose I was jealous,' he grimaced. 'The man seems to have everything. Look at the way Bethany has fallen for him.'

Sian shrugged, tired of everyone talking about Jarrett when she just wanted to forget about him. 'Bethany is very impressionable,' she excused. 'She'll soon get over it.'

'Did you talk to her?'

'Yes, I did.' She frowned at him. 'Does it really matter to you that she's seeing him?'

'She's going to be my sister,' he pointed out moodily.

'Of course. Coming in for coffee?' she offered as they parked outside her home.

'Why not?' he shrugged. 'Oh, by the way, Mum wants you to go over on Saturday. Something to do with the cake, I think,' he dismissed vaguely.

Sian nodded. 'I'll go over after morning surgery.' In the absence of her own mother Sara Newman had been a great help in organising the wedding, even down to making the three-tier wedding cake herself. 'It's probably something to do with the icing of it.'

'I think so,' Chris agreed. 'I never realised a wedding took so much organising.' He followed her into the kitchen, watching her as she made the coffee.

Sian smiled. 'All you have to do is turn up on the day.'

'Oh, I will,' he nodded firmly. 'I wouldn't let you down,' he added grimly.

She paled at his vehemence, her hands shaking as she put the cups in their saucers, her eyes suddenly huge, more green than brown.

'God, I'm sorry!' Chris took her in his arms. 'That was thoughtless of me. Forgive me, Sian.' He looked down at her pleadingly.

'Of course,' she choked, holding on to him tightly, badly needing his reassurance that he loved and needed her—because she needed him so badly at the moment, more than she ever had.

'Darling . . . !' His mouth claimed hers, his lips gentle, his arms strong and protective.

'It would seem we've come in at an inopportune moment!' rasped a glacial voice.

Sian would have sprung guiltily away from Chris like a

criminal caught in the act if he hadn't kept her firmly at his side, his arm like a steel band about her waist. She looked over at Jarrett with widely disturbed eyes, seeing the accusation in his face, the harsh slash of his mouth, the blazing anger in eyes as cold as emeralds.

'Forget the coffee,' Jarrett told Bethany abruptly. 'I'll see you tomorrow.' He turned on his heel, Bethany almost running to keep up with him as he went back to the front door.

'Arrogant swine,' Chris muttered. 'Why shouldn't I kiss you goodnight?'

Jarrett hadn't just been angry, he had been furious, so much so that she knew if he hadn't left when he did he might have resorted to violence, that threat to physically harm Chris rapidly boiling to the surface.

'I'd better go too,' Chris told her regretfully. 'It's late.'

'But your coffee . . .' she reminded him weakly, trembling all over from the fierceness in Jarrett's face.

'I'll take a rain-check,' he said abruptly, kissing her on the forehead. 'Get to bed, darling. It's going to be another long day tomorrow.'

Every day would be long until Jarrett had left Swannell for good. He had acted like a jealous lover just now—and wasn't that what he was? He was her lover now as he had been three years ago, had warned her he wasn't going to stand back and watch her marry Chris. The fact that he had walked out tonight instead of hitting Chris was to his credit; he had never been known in the past for keeping a tight rein on his temper.

By the time Bethany came back into the house, a long ten minutes later, Sian was already in bed, her face blanching as she saw the way her sister's lipgloss was slightly smudged, the starry look in her eyes. Bethany had been thoroughly kissed in the last ten minutes!

'Oh, he's wonderful!' She leant weakly back against the wall, staring dreamily into space.

Sian felt sick at Jarrett's method of retribution at finding her in Chris's arms; she knew by his threats earlier today that he was punishing her through Bethany. It was cruel, cruel and barbaric, like the man himself.

'Don't get too fond of him,' she warned her sister. 'Jarrett never stays in one place for long.'

'He is this time,' Bethany told her happily. 'He's having a house built here.'

'He's *what*?' Sian swallowed hard in her shock.

Her sister gave an ecstatic sigh. 'Jarrett owns some land just outside of town. He told me he's going to build his house there. Isn't that wonderful?'

'Wonderful,' Sian echoed weakly, knowing that now there would be no escaping Jarrett. Ever.

CHAPTER FIVE

She knew exactly where he was going to build his house, knew it, and dreaded it. He had no right to built there. It was their spot, their own private place.

She borrowed her father's car after surgery on Saturday morning, intending to drive over and see Chris's mother. But somehow the car seemed to have a will of its own, driving towards the river, to the place where the weeping willow stood. Sian got out of the car to stand on an elevated position overlooking the fast-flowing water, open countryside every way she looked, the small town of Swannell behind her over the hill. It was a perfect place for a house.

'Sian.'

She turned slowly, feeling no surprise at Jarrett's presence here, half expecting he would join her. It had been inevitable.

She hadn't seen him for two days, although she knew Bethany was still seeing him in the evenings; her sister was as bedazzled as ever by him—much to the worry of their father. Sian knew that she could stop that worry at any time—but at what cost to herself?

Jarrett looked tired, as if he were already weary of the cruel and merciless game he was playing. His over-long fair hair gleamed golden in the sunlight, as did the hair on his arms and chest. His short-sleeved shirt was chocolate brown, unbuttoned at his throat, his denims old and faded as they rested low down on his lean hips.

But his blatant attraction meant nothing to Sian today, her pain was too deep-felt.

'I knew you would come here.' His voice was husky, his gaze intent. 'I knew that eventually you would have to. Bethany told you about the house?' he continued at her silence.

Sian could only look at him, speech impossible. Once she had thought she knew this man, now she realised she had barely touched the surface of the complexities that made up his barbaric nature. He knew what this was doing to her, he had to!

'You remember the house, Sian?' he added harshly as she continued to look at him reproachfully. 'A beautiful colonial-style house, with tall gleaming pillars, vines growing over the walls. An orchard there,' he pointed to one side of the site, 'a swimming-pool there,' he pointed to the other side. 'And the inside of the house will be everything a woman could ever dream of. Two beautiful reception rooms, a huge dining-room, a smaller dining-room for more intimate meals, a pine fitted kitchen. And upstairs there'll be six bedrooms—'

'No!' she protested in an agonised voice, not wanting to hear any more.

'—one for us,' Jarrett continued in a steely voice, his gaze unwavering on her tormented face. 'One for guests. And the other four for the children we're going to have.'

'No!' she flung away from him. 'No . . .' she repeated weakly, her face buried in her hands.

'Yes, Sian,' he spoke softly behind her. 'It's our house, Sian, the way we always planned it. Only now I have more than enough money to make it more than just a dream.' He spun her round to face him. 'Come and live in that house with me, darling,' his voice was husky. 'It's our house, yours and mine.'

Yes, it was their house, the house they had once dreamt of putting here one day as they made love beneath the willow, lying in each other's arms as they planned their future together.

'A farmer owns this land,' she remembered dazedly.

'Not any more,' Jarrett told her with satisfaction.

She blinked. 'But when you asked him before he said he would never sell!'

Jarrett's mouth twisted. 'Everyone has their price,' he shrugged.

Sian's expression was bitter. 'Almost everyone,' she snapped.

He eyed her mockingly. 'But not you?'

'No.'

'You still intend to marry Newman?'

'Yes.'

Jarrett shook his head. 'It will never happen, Sian. When I saw him kissing you the other night it was enough to make me want to tear him apart, limb from limb,' he told her savagely.

'Chris would have fought back,' she told him haughtily. 'He's very strong.'

He nodded grimly. 'I have no doubt he is. And in any other circumstances I could probably like him. But not when I know that each night he's kissing you, touching you,' his voice hardened harshly. 'If I hadn't left when I had, Sian, he would have been nursing some nasty injuries now. You see, I had murderous rage on my side.'

She had known that, had seen it, but it made no difference to her contempt for him. 'Now you have a taste of how I felt when I saw you kissing Nina Marshall,' she scorned.

'I wasn't going to marry her!'

'A pity you didn't tell her that,' Sian bit out tautly.

Jarrett's eyes narrowed to icy slits. 'What's that supposed to mean?'

'It doesn't matter,' she dismissed wearily. 'None of that matters any more. You're really going to build your house here?'

He nodded grimly. 'Exactly as we planned it.'

Sian looked up at him with dull hazel eyes. 'I'll never live in it with you.'

'Oh yes, you will,' he said confidently.

She felt a familiar shiver of apprehension down her spine. 'Jarrett—'

'I love you, Sian.' He pulled her remorselessly towards him, steadily holding her gaze with his. 'The house will be built exactly as we always planned it,' he murmured into her hair. 'And you'll live in it with me, share my bed with me, always be beside me.'

She was weakening again, being seduced by his words and the warmth of his body against hers, her face raised to his as his head slowly lowered and his mouth possessed her.

'I love you, Sian. I love you!' he murmured into her throat minutes later. 'Tell me you love me too.'

Her head was spinning from the warm caress of his lips, her body pulsating with a desire she had no control over, fully under the command of Jarrett's body as he lowered her down on to the grass beneath their feet. And yet she couldn't say those words.

'Tell me!' he urged roughly at her silence.

'I—No!' She flung away from him, her face contorted in misery.

'Tell me, damn it!' He wrenched her chin round. *'Tell me!'* His fingers bit into her arms as he pinned her to the ground.

She swallowed hard, looking up at him with wide frightened eyes. 'Jarrett, please—'

'Please!' he rasped furiously. 'You belong to me, Sian,' he shook her. 'You always have. Do I have to brand you as mine?' he added grimly.

She flinched as she knew what form his 'branding' would take, terrified of the cold glitter in his eyes. 'You would have to force me,' she choked.

'But not for long,' he derided harshly.

Already her body was betraying her, that liquid fire coursing through her veins, a familiar ache in her thighs. She shook her head, holding herself away from him. 'I don't know you like this,' she gasped her distress. 'You—you're frightening me!'

If anything Jarrett looked angrier. 'I'm what you made me, Sian, you with your distrust, your coldness when I tried to explain to you. I might have left you three years ago, Sian, but you had already ruined me for other women. I tried to obliterate you from my senses—'

'With other women?' Her eyes blazed.

'Yes!' he confirmed fiercely. 'But I just used to imagine they were you! I can't begin to tell you how many women have had your face over the last three years. In the end I gave up even trying,' he revealed bitterly. 'No substitute could give me what you can, what you always have. I need you for my sanity, Sian. And I'm going to have you.'

'You told me there had been no other women while you were in America,' she reminded him contemptuously. 'You always were a liar, Jarrett.' She looked up at him fearlessly now, her moment of madness over in the face of his deceit.

His eyes were lit by a blazing fury, his nostrils flaring, his mouth a thin taut line, his fingers biting cruelly into her arms. 'I've never lied to you, Sian,' his voice was dangerously soft. 'There were no "other" women—they were all you, every damned one of them. And they knew that,' he breathed raggedly. 'They knew they were just a vessel of desire for me, that in the morning I wouldn't even recognise them. And I rarely did.' He closed his eyes in self-disgust. 'I've made love to you again and again the last three years, and if you're honest with yourself you'll admit that you sometimes imagine Newman is me. Don't you?' he taunted as he saw the guilty colour in her cheeks.

How could she deny it? She had never done it before, never until the night of Jarrett's return. But that night, that night . . . Yes, it had been impossible for her to do anything else that night.

'You don't deny it, so I know you do,' Jarrett derided. 'You can't marry him and pretend you're making love with someone else. It doesn't work, Sian. Believe me, I've tried it. Only the real thing will do. And you'll eventually destroy Newman if you go through with marrying him,' he warned huskily.

She was beginning to believe that, although she didn't want to, she intended fighting this weakness. She could be a good wife to Chris, if only Jarrett would go away.

She moved completely away from him now, getting slowly to her feet, brushing down her denims. 'I have to go.' She sounded preoccupied, her thoughts troubled.

'Where?' Jarrett stood up to gently remove a leaf from her hair, his fingers lightly caressing her cheek. 'Maybe I could come with you.'

'I don't think so.' Her mouth twisted derisively.

His expression darkened with interest. 'Why not?'

'Because I'm on my way to see my future mother-in-law.'

'Damn you!' he swore forcefully, swinging away from her, his hands thrust into the pockets of his denims. 'You'll never escape me,' he muttered.

Sian wished they could stop hurting each other, but just because he made her confused and troubled about marrying Chris it didn't mean she was going to fall into Jarrett's arms. He was no good for her. Oh, he made her feel wonderfully alive while she was in his arms, but once she was away from him the doubts set in. Jarrett couldn't be trusted to be faithful to any woman, he never would be.

'I have to go.' She turned abruptly, walking quickly to her father's car.

As she slid in behind the wheel she couldn't help looking over at Jarrett. He hadn't moved, but stood staring towards the willow, hunched over, deep in thought, his expression bleak.

Sian reversed down the lane with undue haste, turning the car in a gateway, driving more slowly over the rutted dirt lane until she reached the main road. As she turned the Escort on to the macadamed road she became conscious of the front of the powerful Porsche in her driving mirror, the car looking almost predatory as Jarrett drove it only a couple of feet behind her.

As she continued to drive she knew he was following her, turning the Porsche to the right if she turned to the right, turning to the left if she turned to the left. He didn't believe she was going to see Chris's mother!

Her mouth set rebelliously. Damn him! She accelerated the Escort into town, deliberately driving to the house Chris shared with his parents, parking in the driveway behind Mr Newman's Cortina, turning in her seat as the Porsche purred slowly down the street past the house, doing a U-turn at the end of the cul-de-sac and driving back with speed. Jarrett's expression was stormy as he turned to glare at her.

'Are you going to sit there all day?'

Sian turned to look into the questioning face of Sara Newman. The other woman was an attractive fifty, her dark hair professionally styled, her figure still young and attractive. Both her children took after her in looks, getting their easygoing natures from their father.

'Nice car.' Sara looked shrewdly at the Porsche as the engine no longer purred but roared as Jarrett accelerated it out on to the main road and away from them.

'Yes.' Sian swung easily out of the car, ignoring Sara's curious look and putting her hand in the crook of the other woman's arm. 'Chris said you wanted to talk to me about the cake.'

'Yes, I do. But—'

'Is it the icing?' she prompted as they walked towards the house.

'Yes. But—'

'Tea in the garden—how lovely!' Sian exclaimed with feigned pleasure as she saw the tray laid out on the garden table. 'Hello, Gerald,' she greeted Chris's father as he sat on one of the gaily-coloured garden chairs.

'Hello, love,' he returned sleepily. 'If you women are going to talk about the wedding again I'm going inside,' he grimaced.

'Gerald—'

'Sara, this house has been full of talk about the wedding for weeks now,' he sighed. 'I just wanted to have a nice peaceful afternoon in the garden.'

'Gerald!' Sara gave Sian a pleading look at her husband's bluntness.

Sian gave a light laugh. 'I understand exactly how he feels. Let's just have some tea, shall we?'

'But—'

'For goodness' sake stop saying "but" all the time, Sara,' Gerald told his wife lazily. 'And let's enjoy the peace and quiet.'

With a resigned shrug Sara poured the tea. Sian heaved an inward sigh of relief. The last thing she felt like talking about at the moment was the wedding.

'Maybe we could go into the house and discuss the cake,' Sara suggested a few minutes later. 'As Gerald is feeling so unsociable,' she added crossly.

Her husband's only reply was a sleepy grunt, his eyes closed against the glare of the sun.

'There's no need, Sara,' Sian dismissed, having finished her tea. 'I can come back some other time. There's no rush. When are you expecting Chris back?'

'He didn't say,' Sara shrugged. 'He had to go and take another look at the Jacobs' dog.'

'Yes,' she had known that. 'I'll see him tonight, then. I'd better be going now, I have some shopping to do.'

The other woman looked annoyed by Sian's avoidance of the subject she had supposedly come here to discuss, but she walked down to the car with her, waving goodbye as Sian left to drive home.

Saturday was Bethany's busy day at the salon, and she hurried into the house at six o'clock, refusing food before running up to her room.

'What's wrong with her?' their father frowned.

Sian shrugged, finishing her meal. 'She probably has a date with Jarrett.' In fact she knew her sister was seeing Jarrett, Bethany had seen him almost every night since he had been back in town.

Her father sighed. 'I don't like her friendship with him,' he shook his head.

'I'm sure it won't last,' she consoled—not sure at all!

'Couldn't you talk to her?'

'I have, Dad—'

'Couldn't you try just once more?' he persuaded. 'She'll only end up getting hurt, like you were. The man intends staying here!' he added disgustedly.

Sian could see how worried her father really was, she agreed to go and talk to Bethany, although she knew it would do no good. Bethany was determined to continue seeing Jarrett, and wouldn't hear a word said against him.

Bethany had just finished washing her hair when Sian entered her room, intending to blow-dry it into its usual windswept style. 'Hello,' she greeted breathlessly. 'Sorry, I'm a bit rushed.'

'So I can see.' Sian sat on the bed. 'Going out?'

Her sister gave her a derisive look. 'Isn't it obvious?'

Sian smiled. 'I suppose so. It's just that Dad is—'

'Worried,' Bethany finished. 'I know. But he has no need to be. Jarrett and I are just going to London—'

'London?' Sian echoed sharply. 'That's over fifty miles away!'

'So?'

'So why do you have to go to London?' Sian asked worriedly. 'Darwich is much nearer, and—'

'Not nearly as exciting,' Bethany finished scornfully. 'Jarrett's going to take me to dinner and then a show.'

She frowned. 'But that's going to make it so late.'

'Oh, we're going to stay over—'

'You're *what*?' Sian stood up, her breathing shallow.

Dull colour entered her sister's cheeks, and she avoided Sian's probing gaze. 'Don't be so ridiculous, Sian,' she snapped. 'As you said, it will be late when the show finishes. Jarrett suggested we stay overnight, and I—I agreed with him,' she added defiantly.

Sian chewed on her inner lip. 'You didn't mention this when you came home at lunchtime.'

'That's because I didn't know at lunchtime,' Bethany mumbled.

Sian's eyes narrowed with suspicion. 'What did you say?'

Bethany gave an impatient sigh, putting down the hair-dryer as she gave up the idea of drying her hair for the moment. 'Why do you have to make such a fuss about one night spent in London? In this permissive day and age it's a little old-fashioned, Sian,' she mocked.

'Why didn't you know at lunchtime?' Sian persisted.

'Why?' her sister frowned. 'Because Jarrett only thought of it this afternoon,' she explained. 'He telephoned me at the salon. I thought it was a lovely idea.'

Damn him to hell! He hit her where he knew it would hurt the most. And she was being made to feel every blow, being punished for every slight she might have given him.

'Does Dad know?' she queried quietly.

'Not yet,' once again her sister was evasive. 'I'll tell him before I go.'

'What time is that?'

Bethany shrugged. 'Jarrett said he would be here about seven.'

That gave her time to talk to him, to go to the hotel and plead with him not to do this, to give in to his demands if nothing else would stop his seduction of her sister. He had already taken her pride, she had nothing else to lose!

She smiled tightly. 'I'll leave you to get ready, then.'

'It really is only dinner and a show, Sian,' Bethany's pleading tone stopped her at the door. 'I'm really attracted to Jarrett, but I'm not stupid enough to sleep with him on such short acquaintance.'

'No,' Sian agreed dully, knowing that if Jarrett set out to seduce her sister as he had threatened he would, Bethany wouldn't stand a chance. Jarrett's form of persuasion was lethal!

'I'm really not,' Bethany insisted. 'Jarrett finds me amusing more than anything else.'

'He would hardly turn down the opportunity to sleep with you!' Sian scorned.

'He isn't being given the opportunity,' her sister snapped. 'Don't be such a prude, Sian. Of course I like him to kiss me, but the first man I sleep with is not going to be Jarrett King, fantastic as that experience might be.'

Sian knew Bethany believed what she was saying, and yet she couldn't help feeling sceptical as to her sister's ability to withstand Jarrett. If he wanted Bethany then he would take her. And he would make sure she didn't regret it for a moment. Not at the time anyway. Later it would be a different story, as she had found out to her cost.

'Have a good time,' she told Bethany absently, already planning what she was going to say to Jarrett—after she had told him what a manipulating bastard he was!

'Thanks. Er—you wouldn't tell Dad for me, would you?' Bethany gave her a hopeful look.

Sian gave a rueful laugh and shook her head, seeing how much Bethany dreaded the argument there was sure to be when their father was told of her plans for the weekend. 'I'll leave that to you,' she smiled wryly.

'Thanks!'

She shrugged. 'It's your weekend, Bethany.'

'Yes,' she scowled. 'Okay, I'll talk to Dad myself.'

'Well?' Her father lowered the volume on the television as Sian rejoined him.

'She won't give him up, Dad. In fact—No, I'll let her tell you herself.' Sian bit her lower lip.

'Tell me what?' he frowned darkly.

'Calm down, Dad,' she soothed. 'Bethany will be down soon. She'll tell you then. I—I have to go out myself now.'

'Go out? But—Sian?' he questioned sharply, his frown deepening.

'Don't worry,' she assured him quietly. 'It will all work out for the best—for all of us.'

'But—'

'Please, Dad,' her tone was sharp, 'don't question too deeply.'

He swallowed down his next question, his face dark with concern, watching silently as Sian picked up his car keys and left.

She didn't allow herself time to think, to question, but drove straight to the Swan, intending to talk to Jarrett before he had time to leave to pick up Bethany. She hoped what she had to tell him would mean he didn't go to Bethany at all. And maybe one day Bethany would even thank her for ending her relationship with Jarrett. But not yet she wouldn't.

The Swan was already starting to fill up for the evening when she walked in, a cabaret of a husband and wife singing duo coming on later, but in the meantime there was the bar and the mellow music filtering through the stereo system; the discothèque did not start until much later.

Sian felt very conspicuous as she walked over to the bar that also did as a reception desk for the hotel quests. This was the scene of her humiliation, and it took all her will-power to cross the room in the face of a dozen or so curious stares. It would be all over town by tomorrow that the other Morrissey girl had been visiting Jarrett King at the hotel!

'Sian!' Ida Barlowe greeted her smugly, obviously speculating as to her reason for being here. Sian had rarely been back into the pub since the night of Jarrett's stag party, and never alone, and the fact that she was here now must be food for thought. 'Can I get you anything to drink?' the woman offered.

'No, thanks. I—I'm looking for Jarrett.' Sian cursed herself for sounding like a nervous fool.

Ida frowned, and the music grew louder in that moment. 'I'm sorry, love, what did you say?' There was a vindictive light of satisfaction in the narrowed blue eyes. The Swan's reputation had suffered for weeks from the repercussions of what had become a big scandal in Swannell, and as Sian had helped cause that scandal Ida wasn't one to forgive easily.

Neither was Sian, and she remembered this woman's snubs from the past. 'Is Jarrett King here?' her voice had hardened firmly.

'Mr King?' Ida frowned with feigned puzzlement. 'Wouldn't your sister have a better idea of where he is?'

Sian drew in a ragged breath as the barb hit home—as it had been meant to. 'He isn't here, then?' she said stiffly.

'Well now, I didn't say that—'

'Is he or isn't he?' Sian snapped, tired of this woman's game. She simply didn't have the time to waste on her pettiness.

'No, he isn't,' Ida bit out. 'He went out about a quarter of an hour ago.'

'Oh,' Sian frowned, chewing on her inner lip. That

meant he was already on his way to see Bethany. She was too late!

'If you should happen to find him,' Ida added softly, maliciously, 'perhaps you could tell him Mrs King has arrived.'

The colour left Sian's face in a rush, looking at the other woman open-mouthed. '*Mrs* King?' she repeated dazedly.

'Yes,' Ida confided with relish. 'That's her over there,' she nodded behind Sian. 'She arrived about five minutes ago. So if you *should* happen to see Mr King perhaps you could tell him his wife is here?'

Sian wasn't listening to that spiteful voice any more, but turning to stare at the woman sitting alone at a table a short distance away. The woman was staring back at her, her youthful face exquisitely beautiful, if a little hard, deep blue eyes surrounded by sooty lashes, the beautiful mouth a vivid slash of red, the ebony hair long and silky about her shoulders.

This woman was beautiful—she was also Jarrett's *wife*!

CHAPTER SIX

SIAN felt sick as she stared at the other woman, wondering what sort of monster Jarrett was that he could take Bethany out, could make love to *her*, when all the time he had a wife. He hadn't changed, not at all; he was still the same selfish swine she had walked out on three years ago.

'She's American.' Ida spoke again.

Sian didn't answer the woman, but watched in horror as Jarrett's wife stood up to walk towards her. She was a tall woman, as tall as Sian, moving with a languid grace; the yellow dress she wore was obviously expensive, her legs long and slender, her bare feet thrust into sandals the same shade of yellow as her dress. As she neared Sian she could see that, despite expertly applied makeup, the woman was older than she at first appeared, possibly Jarrett's own age, definitely not much younger.

'Excuse me,' the woman spoke with a softly attractive drawl, her smile friendly, although Sian couldn't help but notice it didn't reach the hard blue of her eyes. 'My name is Arlette King. I couldn't help but overhear you mentioning Jarrett just now. Do you know where I could find him?'

Sian swallowed hard. Something about the woman grated on her nerves, although she couldn't define the feelings. But even so, she couldn't tell this woman Jarrett was out with her sister, she knew only too well how devastating such news could be.

'Miss Morrissey was looking for him herself,' Ida put in, determined not to be left out of what proved to be an interesting conversation.

Shrewd blue eyes were turned on the landlady, and Ida flushed uncomfortably under that icy cold stare. Dark brows were raised as Arlette's returned to Sian. 'Would you like to join me at my table?' she invited silkily.

'I—'

'I would like to talk to you,' she gave Ida a pointed look. 'Alone.'

Sian could see that she wasn't the only one to make an enemy of Ida Barlowe, that this woman had antagonised her without compunction. The Ida Barlowes of this world obviously meant little or nothing to Arlette King; her air of haughty sophistication demanded a certain standard even from this rural public house. And the 'hired help' interfering in a private conversation didn't meet up to that rigid standard.

'Join me for a drink,' Arlette encouraged as she sensed Sian's hesitation. 'Scotch and soda for me,' she requested coolly of Ida. 'Miss Morrissey?'

Sian felt badly in need of something to put the strength back into her limbs, still recoiling from the shock of this woman being Jarrett's wife. He had acted completely without ties since his arrival here, had more than lied when he told her there had been no other woman for him in America, had omitted the fact that he was married, that he had a wife in America waiting for his return. Only she hadn't waited, she had come looking for him! Arlette King looked as if she rarely waited for the things she wanted.

'Sherry, please,' she accepted jerkily. 'Dry.'

Arlette's expression hardened once again as she

looked at the woman behind the bar. 'We will be at my table,' she informed her coldly.

Sian had to admire the way Arlette handled the malicious and inquisitive Ida. The other woman had looked quite deflated by this intended put-down. Although Sian felt uncomfortable as the same hard-eyed stare was directed at her once Ida had brought their drinks a few seconds later!

'Morrissey?' Arlette murmured thoughtfully. 'Your name wouldn't happen to be Sian, would it?'

She gave a start of surprise that the other woman should know this. 'Er—yes.'

'I see,' Arlette nodded.

'Do you?' Sian frowned, not 'seeing' at all herself.

'You were going to marry Jarrett once, weren't you?'

'Was I?' she evaded.

Arlette nodded. 'He told me all about you.'

The sherry Sian had been idly sipping seemed to go the wrong way down her throat, choking her so that she couldn't breathe, and she received a hearty thump on the back from Arlette King as she fought for her breath.

The other woman handed her a tissue from her capacious leather handbag. 'Better now?' she drawled.

Sian dried her tear-wet cheeks, swallowing hard as the choking threatened once again. 'Yes,' she managed to answer in a strangulated voice.

'You don't sound it,' Arlette smiled at her obvious discomfort. 'Didn't you think Jarrett would have told me about you, the woman he had once been going to marry?'

'I—I never even thought about it.' How could she when she hadn't even known he had a wife to tell! She tried sipping her sherry once again, and this time it passed down unobstructed. 'Unfortunately, he didn't give me—us—the the courtesy of telling us about you.'

'That isn't surprising,' Arlette sounded bored. 'I'm not really supposed to be here.' She smiled. 'Jarrett had this crazy idea of coming back here to see the little town he spent several years in, and as I had to stay in Florida to sell the beach-house he probably thought himself free of me for a few weeks.' She looked questioningly at Sian.

Sian couldn't prevent the inevitable flooding of colour to her cheeks, giving her a guilty look when *she* had nothing to feel guilty about. 'He certainly hasn't given the impression of having any—commitments.' She somehow couldn't relate to this woman as Jarrett's wife, although no doubt she suited him perfectly, not seeming in the least jealous, allowing him the sexual and emotional freedom he needed. But why bother to marry at all if that was the way you were going to act? It hardly seemed worth it to her, in fact, it *hadn't* been worth it.

Arlette gave a light laugh. 'Jarrett is impossible, isn't he?' Her smile was indulgent, the rings on her fingers glittering brightly as she raised her glass of whisky to her lips.

For the first time Sian noticed the amount of jewellery the other woman wore—rings on almost every finger, large jewelled rings that had cost a small fortune in themselves, the diamond necklace and matching earrings and bracelet just a bonus.

'And rich,' Arlette drawled mockingly.

Her eyes widened at the other woman's perception of her thoughts. Jarrett was rich, rich enough to provide this woman with all the jewellery she wanted, and his wealth was obviously part of the attraction for Arlette.

'And a wonderful lover,' Arlette added softly.

And that was the other part! Once again Jarrett was

using sex and money to keep something he wanted. And Arlette would be something he wanted to keep, the other woman's sensuality a physical force, more than able to match his own.

'Isn't he, Sian?' she prompted hardly.

'I believe so,' she evaded. 'You'll have to excuse me, Mrs King—'

'Please, call me Arlette.'

'Arlette,' she amended awkwardly. 'I have to get back, I have a date tonight.'

'With Jarrett?'

'No—with my fiancé,' Sian replied confidently.

The shrewd blue eyes levelled on the solitaire diamond ring on Sian's left hand. 'You're engaged?' she said slowly.

'Yes. I shall be getting married next month.'

To her surprise Arlette gave a softly triumphant laugh. 'Poor Jarrett,' she explained her humour. 'How frustrating for him! He intended to resume your relationship, you know,' she answered Sian's questioning look. 'Or didn't you know?'

Sian avoided the other woman's gaze. 'I—'

'You did,' Arlette said with conviction. 'Don't look so concerned, honey. Jarrett's little affairs mean nothing to me. As long as he continues to pay the bills I couldn't give a damn what he does.'

Sian was pale with shock. 'I'm not one of Jarrett's *affairs*,' she said tautly. 'And the—arrangement you have with Jarrett is nothing to do with me.' She stood up. 'If you'll excuse me, I really do have to get back.'

Arlette gave an unconcerned shrug. 'It's been nice meeting you. I intend being here some time, so I'll probably see you again.'

'No doubt,' Sian acknowledged tightly.

She kept her head held high as she left the bar, ignoring Ida's smug expression, her own expression bland until she got outside, then she couldn't hold back the agony any longer, and tears of pain and disillusionment flooded her eyes. She had almost let Jarrett do it a second time, had almost allowed him to ruin her life once again.

Now he had no lever left to pressurise her with. Even Bethany couldn't continue to claim his innocence when presented with his wife! Her sister was going to be hurt, but not as badly as she could have been.

Unless she and Jarrett had already left for London! She should have thought of that, shouldn't have wasted so much time talking to Arlette King. Sian could still be too late for Bethany!

There was no black Porsche parked outside the house when she got there, and her heart sank when she entered the lounge to find her father alone.

'Bethany has already gone?' she queried dully.

'Yes,' her father confirmed grimly.

'Oh.' Sian chewed on her inner lip.

'But not to London,' he added tautly.

Her eyes widened, more green than brown. 'Not to London?'

'No,' he said forcefully. 'To think that a daughter of mine would go off to London with a man like that!' he shook his head disgustedly.

'Bethany changed her mind, then?'

'No, I changed Jarrett's for him,' he told her.

'How?' she frowned.

'By talking some sense into him,' her father said impatiently. 'What does he think it's going to do to Bethany's reputation if it's known she stayed overnight with him in London!'

Sian very much doubted anything her father had to say had changed Jarrett's mind, not when he had been so determined to hurt her. Maybe Jarrett had relented in this plan for revenge.

'He asked about you,' her father revealed reluctantly.

She stiffened, her tone wary. 'He did?'

'Yes,' he sighed. 'I told him you were out for a drive. Although what it has to do with him I just don't know. The man simply can't let go, damn him.'

Yes, damn him. She had been right about Jarrett not changing his mind because of what her father had said to him. Jarrett had guessed the reason for her drive, knew she had been going to see him. He was astute enough to know what her reaction would be to his taking Bethany away for the weekend. How disappointed he must have been that he had left the hotel before she arrived to plead with him. But he had given her her answer to her pleading by his intention to bring Bethany home tonight after all, thought he had finally won. What a nasty shock for him when he got back tonight and found his wife had arrived to spoil everything for him!

Because Arlette King's arrival had freed her; Bethany would stop seeing Jarrett now that she knew he was married, and she—she would marry Chris as planned! Her summer madness was over, Jarrett finally out of her system. It was as if a heavy weight had been lifted, and her love and affection for Chris started to flow again. Jarrett was far out of her reach now, his marriage to Arlette making him so.

She ran over to impulsively kiss her father, laughing as his eyes widened in surprise. 'Poor Dad, no one warned you of the trauma bringing up two daughters could be, did they?' she teased.

'No,' he acknowledged ruefully. 'Although it's had its moments.'

'I can't think when,' she laughed, giving him another hug. 'Chris should be here any minute, I have to go and change.'

'Sian?'

Her father stopped her at the door, and she turned slowly. 'Yes?' she frowned.

'Chris is the better man,' he told her gruffly.

'I know it,' she nodded.

'But we don't always want the things that are "better" for us, do we?'

She shook her head. 'I really do have to go upstairs, Dad,' she murmured softly.

Her father knew! No matter what she told him, how she acted, her father knew that she was once again in love with Jarrett King, that the love she felt for Chris in no way matched the fiery passion she had for Jarrett. It might be wild and destructive, totally unlike the gentler love she felt for Chris, but a part of her would always belong to Jarrett.

It was wonderful to be with Chris that night, more like they had been before Jarrett came back, and when Chris suggested they go to his parents after their meal she readily agreed.

'Feel like talking about the cake now?' Sara asked dryly. 'Sian was too busy to stop this afternoon,' she explained to Chris.

'Were you, darling?' he frowned. 'But I thought you were free all afternoon?'

'I—I was a little late getting here,' she excused, shooting her future mother-in-law a probing glance. Sara was far from stupid, probably knew exactly who the black Porsche belonged to, and no doubt it had made her suspicious.

Sara Newman had always been of the opinion that no woman was good enough for her son, and she made no secret of the fact, which probably accounted for his bachelor state at the age of thirty; Sara had scared off all the eligible females in his life. And she objected strongly to Sian, probably because she had heard of the old scandal, although in that Sian should have been blameless.

But Chris had remained adamant about seeing Sian, being far from a mother-dominated figure, and finally Sara had been forced to accept the situation, and once the engagement became a fait accompli she had set to with a willingness. But that wasn't to say she wouldn't enjoy having it called off, even at this late stage in the preparations.

'Were you delayed with Mr King, dear?' Sara asked casually.

'King?' Chris echoed sharply. 'Did you see King this afternoon, Sian?'

'I—met him quite by chance, in town,' she invented. 'He wanted me to see the spot where he's going to have his house built.'

Chris scowled. 'He's staying on here?'

'Yes,' she answered flatly, all the enjoyment going out of the evening. 'Some of the time, anyway.'

'What do you mean by that, dear?' Sara put in sharply.

Sian looked at her with cool hazel eyes, knowing the other woman had deliberately introduced the subject of Jarrett into the conversation. 'I doubt his wife will want to stay here all the time,' in fact she doubted the sophisticated Arlette would last the week!

'He's getting married?' Gerald Newman seemed to be

having trouble keeping up with the conversation.

'Not—Bethany?' Chris asked.

'No,' Sian frowned. 'He isn't getting married, he already is married. His wife is at the Swan now.'

'Well, I'll be damned,' her fiancé said slowly.

'*He* probably will be,' Sian replied bitterly.

'Where is he going to build his house, Sian?' Sara questioned pointedly.

'Near the river, at Dane's Hill.'

'He'll probably rename it King Hill,' Chris muttered. 'Does Bethany know all this?'

'She knows about the house, because she told me about it—'

'I meant that he's married,' Chris snapped.

Sian frowned at how upset he was. But then Bethany had been like a little sister to him this last year, would soon be his sister-in-law. He was bound to feel a sense of responsibility for her. 'Not yet,' she soothed. 'I thought I'd tell her later tonight.'

'The sooner the better,' he scowled. 'He has some nerve!'

'But why did he follow you here, Sian?' Sara hadn't finished stirring up trouble yet, and was determined to make an issue out of it.

'Follow you?' Chris echoed suspiciously, giving Sian a probing look. 'Did he, Sian?'

'No, of course he didn't,' she dismissed lightly. 'He was coming back to town, he must have followed me thinking he could get there this way.' Even to her own ears it sounded feeble. Damn Sara for stirring up all this just when it looked as if it had all been settled!

'He used to live in Swannell—'

'But only for a couple of years,' Sian insisted stubbornly at Sara's persistence. 'And there has been some new building done since he left. This road never used to be a cul-de-sac,' she added triumphantly. 'Not until they built the new housing estate over the back.'

Sara bit back her annoyance with effort, admitting defeat by the shrug of her shoulders. 'That's true.'

Chris still looked annoyed, his handsome face flushed. 'If they hadn't built that estate we wouldn't need a new shopping centre, and then King wouldn't have come back here.'

'Seems like a lot of ifs and buts to me, son,' Gerald said slowly, eyeing him curiously, surprised at this show of jealousy from his usually calm son.

'Yes.' Chris still sounded disgruntled.

'The cake, Sian?' Sara reminded her of the reason for the conversation in the first place.

'Of course.' She stood up, forcing down her anger with the other woman. She was only protecting her son's interest, after all. 'I brought the bride and groom for the top with me,' she was telling Sara as they went out to the kitchen.

For the next ten minutes they discussed the decoration wanted on the cake, Sara making a lot of the local wedding cakes, her skill known; Sian had no doubt this one would be beautiful.

'I hope you aren't having second thoughts, Sian.'

She looked up into Sara's probing glance. 'And third and fourth ones,' she laughingly dismissed. 'I'm sure all brides have them.'

'You should know!'

The fact that she had been engaged to be married before had been a constant thorn in Sara's side, but Sian could see no benefits to arguing with the other woman about it. She had no doubt Sara would accept her completely once the wedding had taken place; she would have no choice! 'I'm sure Chris has had a few doubts of his own. It's only natural.'

'Is it?'

She was determined not to let Sara's sour mood ruin anything for her, especially her new-found resolve. 'Yes.'

'If you say so,' the other woman said moodily.

Sian could see no further need for discussion—about the cake or anything else. 'Shall we rejoin the men?'

'Of course,' Sara agreed abruptly.

Sian deliberately kept the mood light for the rest of the evening, although she felt some relief when Chris at last offered to drive her home. Sara's mood had been as friendly as her own, and yet she was aware there was still some resentment there; and she had always thought it was the men who had mother-in-law trouble!

The light was on in her father's bedroom when they arrived at her home, and she soon knew the reason her father had gone to bed so early on this Saturday night. The black Porsche was parked in the driveway!

'Damn,' Chris muttered as they got out of the car. 'He and Bethany have been out again, I gather?'

'Yes.' Sian frowned. Obviously Jarrett hadn't been back to his hotel yet. She would enjoy being the one to tell him his wife was here!

Chris sighed. 'It has to stop, you know.'

'I'm sure it will,' she told him confidently.

'Bethany could get hurt.' He scowled. 'Do you think we'll be breaking anything up by going in now?'

She shrugged as he locked the car doors. 'I don't think so.' Jarrett would be basking in his would-be success, would expect her to be meek and submissive, would have little interest in seducing Bethany. He had probably wished the evening over before it had even begun, believing her to be ready to give in to him, to agree to his conditions.

She knew as soon as they walked into the lounge that she was right, saw the flare of triumph in the gleaming green eyes, the mocking quirk to his mouth, although the latter faded somewhat as he saw Chris's arm casually draped about her shoulders.

Sian looked at him with challenge, unable to stop the leap of her senses at how handsome he looked, the brown velvet jacket emphasising the undoubted strength of his shoulders and chest, his shirt snowy white, the dark brown trousers moulded to the lean length of his legs and thighs. His hair was slightly windswept by the gentle breeze outside; Bethany's lip-gloss was perfect tonight, showing she had had nothing to do with the dishevelment of the golden hair.

Sian put her handbag down on the wall unit. 'Did you have a good evening?' She decided to play this casual, aware that the green eyes narrowed questioningly.

'Very good,' Bethany smiled her reply. 'Jarrett took me to this wonderful French restaurant. I even tried frogs' legs!' she revealed with an excited laugh.

'And snails,' Jarrett drawled as Chris seemed to go green.

Bethany grimaced. 'I didn't like them, too garlicky. But the frogs' legs weren't too bad—a bit like chicken.'

'It's disgusting!' Chris grimaced his distaste. 'Barbaric!'

Cool green eyes were turned on him. 'Have you ever tried it?'

'No,' Chris answered defensively. 'But I don't need to to know I wouldn't like it.'

'You can't possibly know that without trying it first,' Jarrett derided. 'Some things can become—addictive.'

Sian knew that the last was directed at her, and decided it was time she put an end to Jarrett's deadly game. 'I think I'll make us all some coffee,' she offered brightly.

'I'll help you,' Jarrett offered instantly.

It was what she had known he would do, knowing he was as anxious to talk to her as she was to him, and privately. As soon as she had seen Bethany's mood of excitement, her infatuation with Jarrett, she had known she couldn't humiliate her sister by telling Jarrett of his wife's arrival in front of everyone. She would derive just as much satisfaction from telling Jarrett privately, in fact more so; she would be able to tell him exactly what she thought of him at the same time!

'Thank you,' she accepted with a sugary smile.

'My pleasure.' His gaze was warm on her parted lips as he joined her at the door.

'Oh, but—'

'Tell me more about this meal, Bethany,' Chris encouraged at her protest. 'It sounds awful!'

'No, it—'

Their conversation drifted off into the background as Sian and Jarrett went into the kitchen. Sian could have kissed Chris for his thoughtfulness, knowing he wanted Bethany to be hurt as little as possible too.

She wasn't prepared for Jarrett taking her into his arms as soon as the kitchen door closed behind them, and she seemed to stop breathing as he ravaged her mouth with a thoroughness that left her weak and gasping.

'You owed me that for this afternoon,' he growled, his hands on her spine moulding her to him.

She held her anger contained with effort. 'I told you—'

'That you were visiting your future mother-in-law,' he finished grimly. 'Only that's no longer true, is it?'

'What do you mean?' she asked with feigned innocence.

'You went to the hotel to see me tonight.'

'Did I?'

His mouth tightened, the warmth of his body scorching her skin, her throat and arms bare in the rose-coloured sun-dress. 'You know damn well you did,' he rasped.

'I went for a drive,' she told him in a puzzled voice. 'And I may have called in at the Swan, but I certainly didn't go there to see you.'

'Sian—'

She pulled out of his arms. 'Yes, Jarrett?' She met his gaze calmly, enjoying watching his puzzlement. Jarrett wasn't usually at a loss, but this time he was. And he didn't like the feeling.

'You came to tell me I'd won, damn you,' he rasped.

Her mouth tightened. 'Won what, Jarrett? Me?' Her brows rose scathingly. 'I was never "yours" to win,' she told him hardly. 'I was never any man's prize,' she bit out angrily.

'And Bethany?' he taunted.

'Ah yes, Bethany,' she drawled fearlessly. 'I think she may change her mind about you soon. And even you might find it hard to take care of both her and your visitor!'

His gaze sharpened, the green eyes speculative. 'What visitor?' he asked softly, almost warily.

And he might well be wary! Sian just hoped he at least felt some guilt when he knew his wife was here. She couldn't believe she had ever loved anyone this selfish.

'Arlette—'

'She's here?' he exploded angrily.

Sian's eyes widened. Jarrett didn't seem to feel guilt at all, he looked furious! His body was suddenly tense, his eyes glacial, his mouth set in a thin angry line. His wife had come all the way from America to be with him and he was angry!

'At the hotel,' she snapped.

'Hell!' he swore viciously, turning away. 'What does she want here?' he spoke as if to himself.

'At a guess,' Sian derided bitterly, 'I would say she wants to see you.'

'Why?' he groaned.

'Well, if you don't know . . .' she taunted pointedly.

'Oh, I know *why* she's here,' Jarrett said harshly. 'I just wondered why it had to be now.'

'Now, Jarrett?' she mocked. 'Messes up your timing a little, doesn't it?'

His mouth twisted. 'Arlette has a way of messing up everything she comes into contact with.'

'How unfortunate for you!'

'It has been in the past,' he nodded grimly, ignoring her sarcasm. 'Did you talk to her?' he asked sharply.

'Not exactly,' she said slowly, watching his frown. '*She* talked to me.'

'Yes?'

Was it her imagination or had Jarrett's wariness increased?

'What about?' he queried softly.

She shrugged. 'You. Her. Me. The beach house in Florida. She's sold it, by the way,' she told him flippantly.

'Good for her,' he drawled uninterestedly. 'Maybe the money from that will keep her happy for a while.'

Sian couldn't believe what she was hearing. Jarrett's

wife had turned up here, and he didn't seem to give a damn—except to wonder when she was going away again! 'Then why do you suppose she's here?' she derided sharply, looking at him with dislike.

'Mm,' he sighed, running a hand wearily through the thickness of his over-long blond hair. 'There is that. I guess the money from the beach-house isn't keeping her happy.'

'She mentioned something about you paying the bills . . .' Sian said with distaste.

He sighed again. 'She has a way of expecting the men in her life to do that. I'll have to go,' he said impatiently. 'She could have shocked everyone at the Swan by now.'

'I don't think so. She seemed a very self-possessed woman to me,' Sian recalled bitterly.

'You didn't like her.' Jarrett sounded amused, his mouth quirked mockingly.

'No.'

'Not many women do,' he smiled his enjoyment of the fact.

'I'm sure with men it's a different matter!'

'Oh yes,' his humour faded, 'completely different. I'm sure even your respectable fiancé would find Arlette attractive—on one of her better days. On the others she's a hellcat,' he said hardly. 'I'd better go,' he repeated. 'I'll talk to you again.'

Sian's eyes widened. 'About what?'

'Us, of course.'

'Us?' she frowned. 'But—Arlette?'

'Is a damned nuisance—and one I intend getting rid of as soon as possible. But she makes no difference to my plans for you and me.'

'*What?*'

'Did you think she would?' He ran a taunting finger

down her cheek, his smile widening as her teeth snapped together angrily. 'No *one*, and *nothing*, will ever make a difference to us, my darling Sian. You may be proving stubborn again now, and I'm sure Arlette's arrival has a lot to do with that, but when the house is finished you'll be the one sharing it with me.' He bent and kissed her hard on the mouth. 'I'll be in touch.'

'Jarrett, you—' Too late, he had already gone!

What did he mean, she would be the one sharing the house at Dane's Hill with him? How could she, when he had a wife—

'Sian, I'm going now.' Chris had come into the kitchen.

'Mm?' She looked up at him dazedly, still shocked by her conversation with Jarrett. It hadn't gone at all as she had thought, there had been none of the guilt from him she had expected, only annoyance that Arlette had come here. And far from putting an end to his pursuit of her he still claimed she would live at the house with him. It didn't make sense—

'Sian, I have to leave now,' Chris repeated curtly. 'I'll see you tomorrow.' He kissed her abruptly.

She shook her head with a puzzled frown, seeing he was already at the door. 'Chris . . . ?'

'Mm?' He turned with a frown, his expression vague.

'Er—nothing.' It had been a long day, maybe it was better if they ended the evening short like this. She needed to think, to be alone, to work out exactly what she had achieved tonight—if anything. Nothing was going right, Jarrett still seemed to want her—and was determined to get her. 'Thank you for a nice evening,' she added huskily.

He nodded, then left quietly.

No one seemed at all interested in the coffee she was

supposed to be making, she thought ruefully. Maybe Bethany wuld like—

'I'm going to bed.' Bethany spoke dully from the doorway.

Sian turned to look at her sister, her eyes widening at how pale she was. 'Love, I—'

'Goodnight, Sian.' Bethany turned with a choked cry, running up the stairs.

Sian watched her go. The whole world was going mad! What on earth was wrong with Bethany? Could—Chris must have decided to tell her sister about Jarrett while they were in the kitchen! Poor love, no wonder she was upset!

She toyed with the idea of going after her sister, then dismissed it. Bethany needed time to get over the shock she had received tonight, time alone.

As no one else seemed interested in coffee she made herself a cup of instant, sitting at the kitchen table to think of her conversation with Jarrett, of *all* her conversations with Jarrett since he had been back.

She had been a fool, had thought each time they spoke that Jarrett was talking about marriage! But marriage was something he hadn't mentioned. He hadn't intended marrying her, he had intended setting her up in his house as his English mistress while his wife continued to live in America!

CHAPTER SEVEN

For the next week Sian saw nothing of Jarrett at all, and neither did Bethany, as far as she knew. Her sister seemed very nervy, snapping at the slightest provocation, spending a lot of time in her room. For the most part Sian left her to it, and by tacit agreement their father did too. When Bethany was ready to talk, to be with them again, she would let them know.

Arlette King was still in Swannell, and Sian occasionally saw her in the town, acknowledging the other woman but making no attempt to stop and talk to her. What could she talk to her about? As far as she knew the only thing they had in common was Jarrett, and they had already spoken of him.

'Sian, where's the Simkins card?'

She looked up with a frown as Chris snapped at her. He had been very snappy lately. She knew it was probably partly due to how busy he had been the last week, seeming to spend a lot of his evenings working late. In fact, they had hardly seen each other out of work since the previous Saturday.

'I put it back in the—'

'How many times do I have to tell you not to interfere?' he scowled. 'I've wasted half an hour looking for the card on my desk—where I left it!'

'But—'

'Just get it for me, will you?' he requested with terse impatience. 'And don't touch the things on my desk again.' He slammed the door behind him as he left.

Ginny softly opened the door to the surgery, putting her head round the side of it. 'Is it safe to come out?' she asked in a stage whisper. 'Has he gone?'

'Yes.' Sian gave a wan smile, finding the card Chris wanted. 'I'd better take this through to him,' she gave a rueful shrug.

Apart from a disgruntled murmur of thanks Chris didn't even acknowledge that she had come into the room. She frowned down at him worriedly. 'Chris—'

'Is it anything important, Sian?' He looked at her with veiled exasperation, his handsome face tight with impatience. 'I want to finish writing up these notes before I go out on my calls.'

'No, I—I—' she moistened her lips. She had never seen Chris like this before. 'I just wondered if you would like to come over this evening? I could cook you a meal and—'

'I'm not sure, Sian,' he answered evasively. 'I could be working again.'

'You've been so busy lately, Chris, and I—'

'I have to work, Sian,' he snapped. 'This practice doesn't run itself!'

'But—'

'I'll let you know later,' he dismissed curtly. 'I really do have to get this paperwork done now.' He turned away.

Sian looked down at him with shadowed eyes for several minutes. She felt hurt and puzzled by his behaviour, had never seen him in this mood before. Finally, when she knew he wasn't going to look up or speak again, she turned and quietly left the room.

Ginny was sitting on top of her desk, her legs swinging idly back and forth as she casually flicked through the picture calendar that stood on Sian's desk. She put it down as Sian came back. 'What's the matter with my big brother?' she frowned.

Sian managed a casual shrug, wondering that herself. 'He's been working hard,' she excused.

Ginny gave a sceptical snort. 'I don't know why.'

'What do you mean?' she frowned.

The other girl shrugged. 'He even took over Martin's turn on call last night.'

Sian kept her expression bland with effort. 'That was nice of him.'

'Nice!' Ginny derided. 'It may have been nice,' she accepted softly. 'I just don't understand why he did it—we weren't going out or anything. Everything is all right between you two, isn't it?' she asked worriedly.

Far from objecting to Sian's marriage to her brother, as her mother did, Ginny openly approved of the match; the two women got on well together.

'Of course,' Sian replied with more confidence than she felt. 'Chris is just trying to get everything organised here for when we get married and go away on our honeymoon.'

'I don't see why,' Ginny frowned. 'He has a replacement arranged for then.'

Sian shrugged. 'He wants to leave everything neat and up to date for him.'

'And that's why he's walking around like a bear with a sore head?' the other girl derided. 'I think there's more to it than that. It's only three weeks to the wedding, isn't it, maybe he's getting impatient,' she grinned.

'Ginny!' Sian's cheeks flooded with colour.

The other girl laughed softly. 'Well, frustration has been known to cause bad tempers you know!'

Sian did know; she had suffered with it herself the day Jarrett had aroused her so thoroughly beneath the willow and she had ended their lovemaking. 'Is that what was wrong with Martin yesterday?' she teased, to hide the confusion she always felt when she thought of Jarrett. She might not have seen him this last week, but just knowing he was still in the town was enough to unnerve her. In fact, she felt more nervous because she hadn't seen him, suspecting his motives.

'That was different,' Ginny spluttered with laughter. 'And that wasn't the reason for his bad mood either. We had an argument about something quite trivial,' she dismissed.

Sian's brows rose mockingly. 'And I thought Martin was the easiest of men!'

'Oh, he is,' his wife nodded. 'But they all have their little foibles.'

'I'm sure,' Sian laughed teasingly.

'You'll see,' she was told prophetically. 'They've started building up at Dane's Hill, you know,' Ginny added conversationally. 'Martin drove past along the main road the other day, he said the building is well under way.'

Sian's smile had faded. 'That's very fast,' she frowned.

Ginny shrugged. 'Jarrett King strikes me as a man who's in a hurry. And when you're a man like him you can arrange anything—especially if you happen to be in the building trade yourself. Martin thinks the house will be finished in a couple of months. I actually saw Jarrett King again the other day,' she went on excitedly, seeming not to notice the strain in Sian's face. 'How on earth could you give up such a gorgeous man to marry my brother?' she asked disgustedly.

'I didn't give him up at the time, Ginny,' she said stiffly. 'I didn't have any choice. He—He was with another woman.'

'So I heard,' Ginny nodded without embarrassment at having listened to the gossip. 'At his stag party. But stag parties are like that,' she dismissed. 'Do you know what they did to Martin at his?' She didn't wait for Sian to answer her. 'They took him out to Darwich,' she named the town five miles away, 'took off his clothes—and left him there. And we got married in March,' she giggled. 'They could have ruined our married life before it began!'

Sian gave an answering smile, never having heard this before. 'Poor Martin! What did he do?' she chuckled at the thought of him stranded without his clothes. How embarrassing for him!

'He telephoned me,' Ginny revealed dryly. 'Reversing the charges, of course.'

'Of course,' Sian grinned.

'And I drove out and picked him up.' Ginny laughed again. 'It was a good job we'd already been lovers, I could have been extremely shocked—or disappointed,' she added mischievously.

'Poor man!'

Ginny sobered. 'I nearly strangled him at the time! You see, shortly before he called me I had another telephone call. From one of his so-called friends, I realised afterwards. He told me that Martin had been found in bed with a married woman and her husband had kicked him out of the house without his clothes.'

'That was cruel,' Sian frowned.

The other girl shrugged. 'It was just fun. I trusted Martin enough to know it was all lies.'

Sian finally realised what point Ginny had been trying to make, turning away. 'Sometimes that trust can be misplaced,' she mumbled.

'Sometimes,' the other girl nodded. 'Is that what

happened with you and Jarrett King?' she prompted softly. 'Stag parties can be a bit wild, you know.'

Sian's mouth twisted. 'This wasn't wild, and Jarrett's party was strictly private.'

'Are you sure? I mean, from what I heard he was mad about you,' Ginny frowned her puzzlement. 'He was the original loner, I've been told, and then there was you.'

Jarrett had been extremely alone. His parents were both dead, and he had only an uncle in America, the majority of friends he made in Swannel after he moved here seeming to be of the female gender. No, as far as women were concerned Jarrett had never been alone.

'There wasn't me, Ginny,' she said exasperatedly. 'There were fifty other women first, *then* there was me.'

'You can't be jealous of his past—'

'It was the present that bothered me,' she insisted heatedly. 'Look, Ginny, don't interfere in things you don't understand. And why stand up for Jarrett King anyway? I'm about to marry your brother!'

'If you aren't over Jarrett King—'

'I am over him!' Sian said fiercely. 'I was over him the minute I saw him with Nina Marshall. I certainly didn't need to be told that he'd been seeing her all the time he'd been seeing me, that he had been sleeping with her too! But I was told, I was told first-hand,' she revealed bitterly.

'I see,' the other girl murmured quietly. 'Sorry, Sian, I didn't realise. And of course I want you to marry Chris. It's just—You don't seem very happy since Jarrett came back.'

'He's stirred up old memories, painful ones, that's all,' Sian dismissed. 'Also it wasn't very pleasant at home while he was taking Bethany out. At least that's over now!'

'Mm, but she doesn't look too happy about it,' Ginny frowned. 'I saw Bethany in town the other day, and she looks awful.'

'She's taken the break-up rather hard,' Sian nodded. 'But I'm sure she'll get over it in time.'

But she wasn't sure at all. Bethany didn't seem to be sleeping or eating; the lunch Sian prepared for her later that day remained almost untouched, as had most of her other meals the last week. She was getting very thin, and having been slender in the first place she couldn't really take the weight loss and still look healthy. But Sian knew there was nothing she could do to ease her sister's pain, that only Bethany herself could do that.

There was no evening surgery that night, and so Sian had the afternoon and evening off, and her disappointment was acute when Chris telephoned to say he couldn't make it that night.

She felt restless, in need of activity, and finally she prevailed upon her father to let her borrow his car, wishing now that she hadn't sold her own car so early before the wedding, even though they had needed the money. She drove out of town, needing to get away from the oppressive atmosphere in the house.

She knew where she was going, of course, knew it and yet couldn't stop herself.

Ginny was right, they had started work on the house. A lot of the building supplies had already been delivered, and several men were still working on the construction as she drove down the dirt road. And one of them was Jarrett!

She didn't need to be any nearer to know it was him, would know that gleaming fair head, naked muscled chest, lean hips in the tight faded denims with her eyes closed. Jarrett was working alongside his men, as filthy dirty as they were—and looking as if he were enjoying every challenging moment of it! This was the way it used to be—Jarrett working long hours, the sweat gleaming on his body, aching with tiredness, and yet glowing with the triumph of a day well used. Tonight he was like the old Jarrett, the impeccably tailored millionaire was nowhere in sight.

By the time Sian had looked her fill of him she was too far up the lane not to have to go to the dead end, past the spot where they were building the house, to the single driveway further down that would allow her to turn around and go back out again.

Jarrett straightened as she drove past the building site, his chest gleaming darkly in the last of the evening sunlight, narrowing his eyes as he recognised her father's car. Sian kept her gaze straight ahead, angry with herself for getting into this position.

She wasn't at all surprised to see him standing in the middle of the dirt lane as she drove back, the dark blue van that had been parked next to the house now disappearing down the lane, leaving a trail of dust behind it. Jarrett must have dismissed his men for the night as soon as he knew it was her in the car!

He didn't make any effort to move as she slowly accelerated the Escort towards him, and she knew that unless she actually wanted to hit him she was going to have to stop. And it was her own curiosity that had once again got her into this situation!

She slowed the car to a stop, winding down the window as Jarrett approached her. Looking at him now was like turning back the clock three years, and she felt her senses leap.

He leant on the roof of the car looking down at her, sweat and dust caked on to his body. 'I was going to have this lane widened and tarmacked,' he said huskily, his gaze intent on her averted face. 'I'm glad now I didn't.'

'Er—Someone told me you had started work on the house,' she shrugged. 'And you have,' she finished lamely.

'Come and take a look.' He was already opening the door, allowing her no chance to refuse. 'Sian?' He held out his hand to her.

She looked at that hand, a roughly calloused hand, dirty now from a day's work, but having the sensitivity to play her body like a finely tuned instrument. Against her own volition, it seemed, her own hand moved into his, her fingers curling around the back of his as his did the same.

'Come and look,' Jarrett urged once again as she hesitated.

She swung her legs to the ground, wearing flat shoes, fitted denims and a fitted shirt, feeling very small next to Jarrett as he guided her through to where they had laid the foundations of the house.

'I had an architect draw up the preliminary plans three years ago—'

'How could you?' she spoke for the first time. 'The land wasn't yours then.'

'It was,' he nodded. 'See, here's the kitchen, over-looking the river and the willow as you always wanted. And over here—'

'Jarrett, you never told me that you owned the land,' she persisted with a frown.

'No. This is the utility room. And—'

'Something else you didn't think to tell me, Jarrett?' Sian rasped with bitterness.

Anger flared in his eyes, a flame burning in the

luminous green depths. 'That's right, Sian,' he bit out tightly. 'Something else I didn't tell you.'

Pain filled her eyes. 'You knew how I loved this spot. You knew how happy I would have been to know *our* spot belonged to you.' Her face was accusing. 'But you didn't care about my happiness, did you,' her voice broke emotionally. 'You owned all this and you—you never said a word!'

Jarrett turned away, his shoulders hunched as he muttered something unintelligible.

'What did you say?' she choked.

He turned fiercely, his hands clenched at his sides. 'I said it was for you. It was to be your wedding gift from me!' he told her savagely, glaring at her as his chest heaved in his deep agitation. 'I was going to give you the deeds to the land on our wedding day, and then we would have planned all this together. *That's* why you didn't know—there wasn't a wedding!'

She swallowed hard, staring at him with pained eyes. Could he possibly be telling the truth, was this really all to have been hers three years ago? Jarrett's anger told her it was.

'I didn't know . . .'

'You weren't supposed to,' he rasped. 'What would be the point of a surprise wedding gift if it were no longer a surprise?' he derided harshly.

She flushed at his rebuke. 'I had nothing to give you—'

'All I wanted was you,' he told her softly. 'Come and see the rest of the house, Sian. I think I've remembered how you wanted it all.'

He had remembered exactly, and he knew he had. It was going to be a beautiful house, a dream house, also a luxurious one.

'Surely you won't need all this, Jarrett?' she frowned

as he showed her where he intended putting the patio and pool. 'Even if you get the building contract here—'

'Which I will.'

'You can't possibly know that. It doesn't come under review until next week, and—'

'I'll get it.'

She knew he would too! 'Well, even *when* you get it, you surely won't be spending enough time here to merit having a house like this built?'

'It's already being built,' he pointed out dryly. 'And even without the building contract this is going to be my home in future; I've only a few last things to move over here before King Construction is English based.'

'Doesn't Arlette have something to say about that?' she taunted.

He shook his head, his expression grim. 'Arlette has no say in my life.'

'I doubt if she'll like living here,' Sian scorned.

'She isn't being asked to! She's messed up my life long enough, when she goes back to the States she stays there.'

She swallowed hard. 'She won't be living with you?'

'God, no! As soon as she's got the money out of me that she wants she'll go back to New York and stay there. She's always liked the apartment in New York. You know damn well she wouldn't be living in this house, Sian,' he snapped. '*You* will.'

'No—'

'Will you just *stop* this!' He completely lost his temper with her. 'You've put me through enough. I'm not going to beg, Sian. This is our house, and *we* are going to live in it.'

'I think Chris might have something to say about that,' she taunted.

Jarrett's mouth tightened at the mention of the other man. 'Aren't you leaving it a little late to tell him the wedding is off?'

She turned away. 'But it isn't.'

'Damn you, Sian—'

'Swearing at me won't change anything, Jarrett. I couldn't trust you before, and events have proved I would be a fool to trust you now.'

'Events?' His eyes were narrowed. 'What events? Do you mean my seeing Bethany?'

She shook her head. 'There was Nina in the past, and there's Arlette now.'

'Arlette means nothing to me—'

'Then I feel sorry for you,' she glared at him, her face flushed. 'You use and discard women like you would a—a shirt,' she said exasperatedly. 'I'm going now, Jarrett. I really hope you don't stay in Swannell!' she turned to walk away.

He wrenched her round, a cold glittering fury in his face. 'You aren't going anywhere, Sian, not until I've talked some sense into you. It isn't just your own life you're ruining by your stubbornness, your unwillingness to see the truth, that you belong to me. There are too many people involved, Sian, some of them just innocent bystanders.'

'Like Bethany!'

'And Newman,' he bit out gruffly. 'He means nothing to you. Oh, you care for him, I don't think you could marry anyone you didn't care for—'

'Thanks!'

'But there's a difference between caring for someone and loving them.' He grasped her arms, holding her firmly in front of him, one hand wrenching her chin up, forcing her to look at him. 'Look me straight in the eye and tell me you don't love me,' he ordered roughly.

She was conscious of his heated warmth, of his physical attraction reaching out for her, pulling her towards him, and the groan in her throat was one of submission, her gaze softening, her moistened lips parted invitingly.

'You know I love you, Sian,' Jarrett moaned. 'Why else would I be here?'

'The hotel and shopping centre—'

'Don't be ridiculous,' he snapped. 'King Construction Company is vast, I have men on site who deal with things like that.'

'And this house?'

'Is a labour of love,' he told her without hesitation. 'I always intended to build this house for you. I wish now that I'd arranged for it to be done before I came back, then I could have moved you straight in and there would have been none of this fighting me all the time.'

Sian pulled away from him with a disgusted snort. 'Your arrogance knows no bounds, does it? You think you only had to come back here and snap your fingers and I would come running!'

'I've asked you to come to me, Sian,' he reminded her grimly. 'I haven't demanded.'

'Maybe that's as well!'

'I'm beginning to think not,' he bit out. 'I thought you had enough sense, knew *me* well enough, to have ended things with Newman by now. You're just prolonging the inevitable.'

'I have to go—'

He sighed, pulling on the light green shirt he must have discarded earlier in the heat of the day, but making no effort now to button it. 'Drive me back to town, will you?'

Anger flared in her eyes at his dictatorial tone. 'I—'

The Porsche roared into view down the dirt lane, dust spiralling into the air as it was driven with great speed down the totally unsuitable lane, Arlette King sitting behind the wheel.

Sian's mouth tightened. 'You must have forgotten you'd already *asked* to be picked up.'

'Damn her to hell!' he swore as the Porsche came to a screeching halt feet away from them. 'That's no way to handle a sensitive piece of machinery,' he was scowling heavily as he marched over to where Arlette was just sliding out from behind the wheel. 'What do you think you're doing?' he rasped furiously. 'This isn't Brands Hatch, you know!'

'Don't be so bad-tempered, Jarrett,' Arlette told him without concern, her hand on his arm. 'Miss Morrissey,' she greeted coolly before turning back to Jarrett. 'Honey, you surely haven't been talking to Miss Morrissey dressed like that?' she derided his still bared chest.

'She's seen a damn sight more of me than this,' he still scowled.

Arlette gave a throaty laugh as Sian blushed. 'You're always so physical, Jarrett!'

'I have to go,' Sian told them abruptly.

'Sian—'

'Jarrett, I'm longing for my dinner,' Arlette told him softly. 'I've been waiting for you.'

His gaze was fixed on Sian. 'I didn't ask you to,' he told the other woman callously. 'Join us for dinner, Sian?' he invited huskily.

She almost choked at the gall of this man. He cared nothing for the fact that his wife was clinging to his arm, at how obvious he was making his desire for *her*. 'No, thank you,' she said tightly. 'I really do have to go. I hope you enjoy living in the house when it's finished, Mrs King,' she added with spite for Jarrett.

'I wouldn't live in this godforsaken hole if I were paid to,' the other woman scorned.

'I might pay you to go away, but never to *stay*,' Jarrett told her with blunt cruelty.

Arlette's smile was tight. 'Careful, honey,' she drawled throatily. 'You'll give Miss Morrissey the impression we don't get on.'

'We don't!' he rasped coldly.

'No, but we're stuck with each other, aren't we?' Hard blue eyes glittered her hatred of him.

'For the moment,' he acknowledged tightly. 'But my lawyers are working on that.'

Arlette smiled without sincerity. 'It could take years without my co-operation,' she taunted.

'It will be worth it!'

Sian had heard enough, and turned with a choked cry to get into her father's car and turn on the ignition.

Jarrett reached her before she could drive off. 'I'm sorry,' he said abruptly. 'Arlette and I shouldn't have aired our differences in front of you.'

'No.' She stared rigidly in front of her. She had very much doubted the success of Jarrett's marriage, but that there was so much bitterness and dislike between them she hadn't guessed.

He sighed his frustration. 'Why is it I never seem to finish a conversation with you?'

'Because we always talk about the same subject,' she said coldly. 'And you never like the answer I give you.'

His eyes flared with anger. 'Not until you change your answer to yes,' he ground out.

'Arlette is getting impatient for her dinner.' She put her foot down on the accelerator pointedly.

He moved back from the car. 'Suddenly I'm not hungry,' he grimaced. 'Why won't you join us, Sian?'

'Because I'm not hungry either. And neither do I care for the company!' She accelerated the Escort down the lane, not sparing another glance for either Arlette or Jarrett.

She could feel no sense of elation that Jarrett's marriage was such a disaster, wasn't bitter enough of his betrayal of her to be that insensitive. It sounded as if the two of them would be divorcing, although that still didn't lessen the outrage of Jarrett's proposition towards her.

Her father had fallen asleep in the chair when she got home, although he woke up as she came into the lounge. 'Blown the cobwebs away?' he sat up with a tired yawn.

'Just about,' she nodded, giving him back his car keys. 'Is Bethany still upstairs in her room?'

Her father shook his head. 'She went out about half an hour ago. One of her friends called, she went out with them. It will do her good.'

'Yes,' Sian agreed, glad that her sister was at last going out again. And she knew it wasn't with Jarrett, because she had been with him herself half an hour ago. And he was with his wife now.

'You aren't seeing Chris at all tonight?' her father frowned.

'He's busy,' she shrugged.

'Is that all it is?' her father probed softly.

She grimaced. 'I think he's still annoyed about Jarrett being here.'

'But that isn't your fault. Or is it?' his gaze sharpened. 'I've heard that he's building his house on Dane's Hill?'

'Yes,' she nodded.

'Where the two of you used to meet.'

'Yes.' Even to her own ears she was beginning to sound strained now.

'The man either has no emotions at all—or too much,' her father added thoughtfully.

The bright colour in her cheeks seemed to be a permanent fixture. 'That doesn't make much sense, Dad,' she attempted brightly.

'Of course it does, Sian. Jarrett either feels nothing for you and the past—or he cares too much to let go.' Her father's gaze was searching. 'I think, knowing him as I did, that it's the latter. Am I right?'

She turned away, shrugging. 'How would I know?' she dismissed carelessly.

'All too easily. Jarrett was always a blunt man. If he had something to say then he said it. Has he spoken to you about his feelings since he came back, Sian?'

'Even if he has it won't do him any good.' She was becoming agitated. 'I think I'll have an early night, Dad. We have to be up early in the morning to go to church. Mr Small expects us there to hear the banns being read.'

'You're still sure about marrying Chris?'

She frowned. 'Why do you ask me that?'

'Because this whole household has changed the last week and a half since Jarrett came back. Bethany's like a ghost, you're jumpy all the time, Chris has suddenly developed moods. If you're having second thoughts about marrying Chris—'

'I'm not. I've never been so sure of anything in my life,' she said stubbornly.

'Haven't you?' her father chided softly. 'I seem to remember a bright-eyed, ecstatically happy young lady telling me that once before.'

Her blush deepened. 'I made a mistake that time.'

'Did you? Perhaps,' he nodded. 'But you looked a damned sight happier then than you do now.'

'Until it ended,' she reminded him bitterly.

'Life isn't all happiness,' he shrugged.

'With Jarrett it wouldn't have been happy at all!'

'You think you stand a better chance with Chris?'

'I'm sure of it!'

'I just want what's best for you,' he told her gently.

'I know you do, Dad,' her mood softened. 'I'm sorry I was so snappy. It's always a tense time before a wedding.'

He nodded. 'I'll come to church too in the morning.'

'I'd like that.'

In the end only her father accompanied her to the service. Chris was called out to an emergency at the last minute, and Bethany was still in bed. Her sister had got in very late the evening before, and when Sian had gone to the bathroom at two o'clock this morning her sister's bedroom light had been on, although her gentle knock on the door received no answer. Not wanting to intrude, she had gone back to her own room.

The church was very full when they arrived slightly late, and Sian and her father slipped into a pew at the back, her breath catching in her throat as she looked up to see Jarrett strolling in behind them with long powerful movements, his narrow-eyed gaze flickering around the church, going past Sian only to come back again as he recognised her.

She instantly looked towards the altar, very conscious of the bareness of the pew beside her.

It was inevitable, of course, obvious that Jarrett was going to sit beside her, his thigh deliberately resting against hers in the confined space.

She stared straight ahead, very conscious of the bent

blond head beside her, of the way her father glanced past her at the other man, his brows raised at her in query. She simply shrugged her tightlipped reply; she had no idea what Jarrett could possibly be doing here either.

The whole of the service was an agony for Sian, although Jarrett seemed perfectly relaxed—until it came to the end when the notices were read out! Then his whole demeanour changed, his eyes hardening, his face tight with tension, his mouth thinning, his body tense with anticipation.

As the vicar read out the banning of her marriage to Chris in three weeks' time Sian saw Jarrett blanch, and she suddenly knew the reason he was here. He had come to see if she had gone through with having the banns read!

CHAPTER EIGHT

SIAN wished her father would hurry up; Jarrett was talking softly with the vicar at the moment, but his gaze was fixed on her as she nervously waited for her father to stop talking to one of his bowls cronies. She had driven here with him, she couldn't very well leave without him. But she didn't like the way Jarrett was staring at her; she felt as if his gaze burnt into her.

People were standing about the churchyard chattering in groups. Several other men had joined her father now, which meant he wouldn't be ready to leave for some time yet.

'I'll be here next week too, Sian,' Jarrett spoke softly behind her. 'And the week after that too. And on your wedding day I shall stand up and tell everyone that I'm a very "just cause" why you shouldn't marry Newman.'

Sian turned sharply at the threat in his voice. 'You can't do that!'

His teeth were very white against his tanned skin as his mouth twisted in a facsimile of a smile. 'Try me.'

'Why would you want to ruin my life a second time, Jarrett?' she asked wearily, stiffening as she saw Sara Newman watching the two of them with interest. She had known the other woman was to be here, had intended meeting her before the service if she and her father hadn't been late arriving. This was all she needed after Sara's previous suspicion over Jarrett!

He followed her line of vision. 'Newman's mother,' he realised.

'Yes,' she acknowledged.

Jarrett shrugged dismissively, his shoulders broad beneath the brown suit and tan shirt he wore. 'I don't intend ruining your life, Sian,' he told her deeply. 'You seem to be the one intent on doing that. Where's Newman today?' he rasped.

'Working,' she said abruptly.

'On a Sunday morning?'

She flushed at his scepticism. 'He's a busy vet.'

'I'm a busy man myself, Sian. But I could always make time for my beautiful fiancée.'

'And Nina. Don't forget Nina,' she derided harshly.

'I wish to hell you would—'

'Would you please lower your voice,' she muttered softly, a falsely bright smile on her face as several people turned to look in their direction.

'Frightened your future mother-in-law might hear?' he ground out.

'Yes! Please, Jarrett,' she looked at him with appealing eyes. 'When you're tired of this game you're playing I'll still have to live here!'

'You'll be with me,' he shook his head. 'Wherever I happen to be.'

'I wouldn't leave with you before, Jarrett, and I won't this time either!'

'You—'

'Ah, Sian,' Sara joined them, smiling enquiringly at the tension that surrounded them. 'We missed you earlier. How nice to meet you at last, Mr King.' Her voice hardened.

'Mrs Newman,' he returned smoothly, all anger gone from his expression and manner. 'I can't tell you how much I'm looking forward to your son's wedding next month,' he drawled.

'Thank you,' Sara accepted tightly. 'It should be a beautiful wedding.'

He nodded. 'I always thought Sian would make an exquisite bride.'

'No doubt.' Sara's manner was even stiffer.

'Well, if you'll excuse me, ladies,' he said politely, 'I have to get back to my hotel. I have an appointment for lunch.'

And Sian didn't need two guesses who his appointment was with! 'Don't let us keep you,' she said with exaggerated sweetness, aware that while he hadn't actually said anything impolite to Sara his words had been offensive nonetheless.

'Mrs Newman,' he nodded. 'Sian,' his voice filled with warmth as he paid her back for her sarcasm.

And it did; she could see Sara's speculation had increased, watching Jarrett as he walked away. 'Fascinating man,' Sara murmured.

'I suppose so,' Sian nodded, chewing on her bottom lip.

Sara swung hard blue eyes back to her. 'Wasn't he a little old for you?' she frowned. 'Even then?'

'Perhaps, I never really thought about it.' Sian turned away. 'Ah, here comes Dad,' she smiled. 'Will Chris be coming over for lunch or is he still working?' she asked the other woman.

Sara frowned. 'He didn't come with you?'

Sian shook her head. 'He rang to say he had to go out on a call.'

'Strange,' Sara said slowly. 'I don't remember—Oh well, I suppose he'll be over to see you some time today. You mustn't begrudge the time he spends at his work, Sian. He's building up the practice for your future, for both of you.'

'Oh, but I—' She didn't get a chance to defend herself any further, for her father joined them, although she burned with indignation at the criticism. She had never complained about the long hours Chris worked, had always understood the demands of his career.

'Strange woman,' her father remarked on the drive home. 'Can't understand what Gerald sees in her.'

'Dad!'

'But I can't,' he shook his head. 'And it isn't natural to cling on to your children the way she does.'

Sian gave a teasing laugh. 'You just can't wait for the day you can throw Bethany and me out!' she mocked.

'I'm gaining a son—she doesn't even want another daughter. Thank God you aren't going to live there after you're married!' he grimaced.

'I couldn't,' she shook her head. 'Sara and I will never get on except from a distance, whereas you and Chris get on very well together.'

'Not so much lately,' he sighed. 'I always thought he was the least moody person I knew, but this last week . . . !' He shrugged. 'He hasn't been himself at all.'

She knew that, and no matter what she said to the contrary, Chris's behaviour did bother her. He was usually so open, so even-tempered, and this last week he had been anything but that—completely unapproachable at times.

And she was to blame for that, she knew she had to be. Chris must sense the indecision within her and resent this upset to their plans at this late stage of things. It was up to her to show him that he was the one she cared for, the one she intended marrying and sharing her life with.

She was pleased to see his car parked outside the house when they arrived home, smiling brightly as she entered the lounge. Chris and Bethany were talking heatedly as she walked into the room, although they fell silent as Sian and her father came in.

With a choked cry Bethany turned and fled the room, while Chris glowered angrily.

'What's going on here?' Sian's father frowned. 'What's wrong with Bethany?' he questioned Chris roughly.

The younger man thrust his hands moodily into his pockets. 'I seem to have upset her,' he stated the obvious.

'I can see that,' the other man growled. 'I want to know how.'

Chris shrugged. 'She took exception to something I said.'

'About what?'

'We were just talking, and I—I just said something I shouldn't,' Chris dismissed.

'You didn't criticise Jarrett, did you?' Sian chided gently. 'You know how upset she's been about him this past week.'

'King?' he frowned. 'But I—Well, I didn't know it would upset her that badly.' His brow cleared.

'Never mind, darling,' Sian touched his arm comfortingly. 'I'll go and talk to her.'

'No! Er—no,' he softened the sharpness of his tone. 'Maybe it would be better to leave her alone for a while. I'll apologise to her the next time I see her.'

She thought for a moment. 'Maybe that would be best. I'll just go and check on lunch,' she suggested brightly, reaching up to kiss him lightly on the mouth. 'I'm glad you came over, darling.'

He gave a tight smile. 'Yes.'

'Like a cup of tea, Dad?' she offered.

Her father was still puzzled by Bethany's outburst. 'Yes—thanks,' he replied absently.

All was silent upstairs as Sian went to the kitchen. Poor Chris, he couldn't possibly have known the hornets' nest he would upset by criticising Jarrett to Bethany. It seemed a pity it had had to happen, as the two of them had always got on so well together. She shrugged philosophically. Once Bethany was over her feelings for Jarrett she would see that Chris had only been thinking of her welfare in his advice.

She really was glad Chris had managed to finish in time to join them for lunch; she had missed him this last week. And if she were honest with herself, she needed to be with him; once more she was feeling unsettled by Jarrett's persistent presence in her life.

She and Chris went out for a drink together Tuesday night, and she had no objection when Chris suggested they go to the Swan; she had no intention of hiding from anyone.

'I hear King got the contract for the hotel and shopping centre,' Chris remarked conversationally.

'Yes.'

'You knew?' His dark brows rose.

'I—heard.'

'From King himself?' His mouth twisted.

'No—of course not,' she faltered. 'Your father mentioned it to me last night.' Chris's brusqueness hadn't improved the last couple of days, if anything it had worsened.

He scowled. 'I only found out today.'

'Does it matter?'

His eyes narrowed. 'I don't know—does it?'

'Not to me,' Sian dismissed evasively.

'My mother said you were talking to him again on Sunday.'

She might have known Sara wouldn't miss that opportunity to cause trouble! 'Talking to him, yes.'

'Sian—'

'Good evening, Sian. Newman.'

They both turned at the sound of that silky voice tempered with steel, looking up into Jarrett's cold green eyes.

'Jarrett,' Sian said awkwardly, while Chris said nothing at all, but eyed the other man moodily.

Only Jarrett looked relaxed out of the three of them; he was casually dressed in a light blue shirt and denims, standing close to their table. 'I haven't seen the two of you in here before.'

She shrugged, while Chris was still noticeably silent at her side. 'We rarely come here.'

'I wonder why,' he drawled mockingly.

Chris did look up now, his expression belligerent. 'Sian and I usually have better things to do with our time than sit drinking in pubs!'

'Indeed?' Jarrett met his anger with coldness.

'Yes!' the other man glared at him.

'Congratulations on the new building contract, Jarrett,' Sian rushed into speech, not wanting to cause a scene here. Ida Barlowe had already had quite enough gossip about her, without adding to it!

'Thanks,' he nodded coolly.

'You must be pleased.'

'Very,' he nodded. 'But like I told you, I expected it,' he said without conceit.

'Why?' Chris sneered. 'Did you cross a few sweaty palms with silver?'

Sian gasped, her gaze flying to Jarrett's furious face.

He was a lot of things, but he certainly wasn't dishonest! She couldn't think what had possessed Chris to talk in this way, it wasn't like him at all.

Jarrett looked at the younger man with cold green eyes. 'I believe your father is one of the Councillors who made the decision about the contract,' he said pointedly.

Chris's head went back in fury. 'And what's that supposed to mean?' he ground out.

Jarrett gave an unconcerned shrug. 'Work it out for yourself,' he drawled.

'Why you—'

'Please, Chris,' Sian put her hand on his arm as he went to stand up, his face contorted with rage. 'I'm sure Jarrett wasn't implying anything. Please, darling,' she urged as she could still feel his tension beneath her hand.

She heard Jarrett's sharply indrawn breath, and looked up to find the dangerous glitter of his gaze fixed on the way she was touching Chris's arm. Not now—he couldn't show his own jealousy now! She felt as if she were being pulled apart by the two of them, feeling her confidence wane and crumble, knowing that if these two men wanted to be at each other's throats, and it seemed that they did, she wouldn't be able to stop them.

Chris seemed to subside at her side. 'If you say so,' he mumbled.

Just as she was about to start breathing again she sensed Jarrett's unrelenting attitude. His gaze was still fixed on her hand on Chris's arm, and she hastily removed it.

But not quickly enough. 'If you have something to say, Newman, then say it,' Jarrett rasped, his gaze swinging back to the other man. 'If you think I "fixed" the building contract for King Construction Company then perhaps you ought to ask your father about it.'

'There's no need for that,' Chris snapped.

'No?' the other man taunted.

'No!' Chris stood. 'I think it's time we left, Sian.'

'But—'

'If you aren't ready yet,' he glared down at her with fierce blue eyes, 'I'll wait outside in the car.' He pushed past Jarrett and marched out of the pub.

Sian made to follow him.

'No,' Jarrett grasped her wrist to stop her leaving. 'Let him go,' he ordered grimly.

Her eyes were swimming with tears as she looked up at him. 'What are you trying to do?' she choked.

'What am *I* trying to do?' he scorned. 'Your *fiancé* more or less accused me of bribing my way into that building contract.' His voice hardened.

'I'm sure Chris didn't mean—He's been a little tense lately, and—and—well, you did get the contract against all the odds. A couple of local builders put in for it. It was expected one of them would be awarded it.' Jarrett had begun shaking his head before she had even finished. 'No?' she arched her brows.

'No,' he confirmed.

'How could you know that?' she frowned.

'Because I had to get that contract.'

'But how did you—'

'By putting in the lowest costs,' he shrugged.

'That's obvious. But—'

'The rock-bottom costs,' he explained grimly.

'You mean you—But why, Jarrett?' she gasped.

He sighed heavily. 'When I saw the announcement of your engagement I knew I had to come back as soon as possible, but I needed a reason to come back, hence the contract. Once I arrived here I realised I didn't have the time for that, that your wedding was too close to waste any more time. I decided to let the bid for the contract go ahead, but to use a more direct approach on you.'

'I noticed,' she derided. 'Well, the fact that you intend being in Swannell for some time is up to you. Maybe if you're still here when Chris and I get back from our honeymoon we'll invite you over to the house for dinner.'

'Like hell you will!' his expression darkened. 'Maybe we'll invite him, *not* the other way round.'

'I'd better go.' She looked past him as Arlette stood framed in the doorway. 'You have company.'

He glanced only fleetingly at the other woman. 'She can wait,' he dismissed.

Anger flashed through her. 'Maybe one day she'll get tired of waiting and walk out on you.'

'I can't wait for the day!'

'You really are an unfeeling bastard!' She shook off his hold on her wrist.

'Jarrett!' Arlette had joined them now. 'And Sian,' she looked at her with mocking eyes. 'My, how I do seem to keep running into you! And always with Jarrett,' she mused, putting her arm through Jarrett's. 'Why is that, honey?' she asked him throatily.

'Mind your own damned business!' he scowled.

'But it is my business,' she purred. 'Everything you do concerns me. Or have you forgotten?' she taunted.

'I've forgotten nothing where you're concerned,' he bit out grimly. 'Not Frank, not the affairs. I want you back in New York, Arlette. And I want it soon.'

Dark brows rose over hard blue eyes. 'Is that any way to talk to me, honey?' she mocked. 'Especially when you know I have no intention of going back to New York without you. I like you where I can see you.'

'And I like you where I *can't* see you,' he returned callously, turning on his heel and leaving the room.

'My, my,' Arlette drawled. 'That's two men who've walked out on you in one evening, Sian.'

She stiffened at the taunt, sensing that the gloves were definitely off. 'You saw Chris leave?'

The other woman nodded. 'I even tried to talk to him. He was very uncommunicative,' she added dryly.

'I have to go—'

'I should,' Arlette nodded. 'I would also stay away from Jarrett in future. He can be very cruel when he wants to be.'

'I have no reason to suppose he would ever want to be with me,' she said coldly.

'Jarrett's only nice when he wants something,' Arlette warned. 'Once your usefulness is over, in this case when he tires of you in his bed, he'll discard you without a qualm.'

'Is that what happened to you?' Sian snapped.

Dull colour flooded Arlette's cheeks. 'You little bitch!'

'Then that makes two of us,' she sighed. 'Goodnight, Mrs King.'

The length of time she had been delayed in the Swan she quite expected Chris to have left without her. But his car was still in the car park, and she climbed quickly into the passenger seat beside him.

He turned on the ignition with an impatient flick of his wrist, driving steadily to her home, not saying a word.

'Chris, I—'

'Please, let's not talk about it, Sian,' he said abruptly. 'I behaved like a fool, we all know that. It's hardly King's style to use influence in a little contract like this one in

Swannell. He hardly needs the money such a small venture would give him!'

'No,' she acknowledged softly.

Chris sighed. 'I suppose I'll have to apologise to him too. I seem to be upsetting everyone lately.'

'You've seen Bethany?' She changed the subject from Jarrett, amazed at the lengths he would go to get her back—and disgusted with the way he had spoken to his wife. She didn't like Arlette King, but she hadn't enjoyed seeing her humiliated in that way.

'Yes,' Chris answered abruptly. 'Yesterday. After work.'

'She didn't mention it.'

'No?'

'She still spends a lot of time up in her room,' Sian frowned.

'So I believe.'

She chewed on her bottom lip. 'I wish there were something I could do to help her.'

'Don't interfere in her problems, Sian,' Chris snapped. 'She's a big girl now, old enough to decide her own life. And she won't thank you for your advice.'

'But I—'

'Just leave her alone, Sian!'

She was taken aback by his vehemence. Chris was in a really strange mood lately, one she didn't understand, and one that she wasn't sure she liked either. She hardly knew him like this, and it made her nervous.

'I've done it again, haven't I?' he sighed a few minutes later. 'I'm sorry, Sian, I shouldn't have shouted at you.'

'Is everything all right, Chris?' she frowned. 'At home, and at work?'

'Yes, of course,' he answered tersely. 'I can't be in a good mood all the time, Sian,' he added abruptly.

She wanted to ask why he couldn't, but thought better of it. He had a very successful career, a career that he loved, and they were going to be married in two weeks' time; that should have been enough to make any man happy.

He refused to come in for coffee, and she didn't pressurise him, sensing his urgency to leave; their kiss goodnight was short and sweet.

Sian was frowning heavily as she entered the house, although her expression brightened as she saw Bethany sitting in the lounge with their father. Her young sister seemed to have been avoiding her wherever possible lately, and it made a pleasant change for the three of them to spend a little time together.

Her father looked at his wrist-watch. 'You're early, love,' he said slowly. 'It's only ten o'clock.'

She shrugged. 'Chris was feeling tired.'

'He's working too hard,' her father shook his head.

'Yes,' she answered absently. 'Hello, Bethany,' she greeted gently.

'Hello,' her sister returned abruptly.

Their father frowned at them worriedly. 'I think I'll go to bed.' He stood up.

Sian frowned. 'No coffee?' She had never known her father to retire for the night without his cup of coffee.

He smiled. 'I'll go and make some. Anyone else?'

The two girls shook their heads, and he went off to the kitchen whistling softly to himself.

Sian knew that her father had deliberately left them alone, also sensing Bethany's awkwardness with her. 'Is the film any good?' she sat down.

Her sister gave an uninterested shrug. 'I haven't been watching it.'

Sian chewed on her bottom lip, undecided about

Bethany's mood. The younger girl had been so adamant about Jarrett, it must have been very humiliating for her to discover everything Sian had said about him was true. She knew that part of Bethany's coolness towards her lately was out of embarrassment for those predictions coming true, and she wasn't sure if Bethany was ready to forgive her for that yet.

Bethany suddenly stood up. 'I may as well go to bed too.'

'Bethany—'

'Hm?' Her sister seemed to stiffen.

'I—I'm sorry about Jarrett,' she said almost appealingly. 'I didn't think he would turn out quite as bad as he has.'

'Jarrett?' Bethany looked startled.

'Yes,' she chewed on her bottom lip. 'He treated me badly, but I had no idea he would so callous with you too.'

'I don't know what you mean,' her sister said distantly. 'I haven't been seeing Jarrett, but it's from my own choice.'

Sian could see this was a matter of pride with Bethany, and she didn't push the subject any further. 'How is work?' she asked interestedly.

'The same as always,' her sister shrugged, feigning a yawn. 'I'll see you tomorrow, Sian.'

Sian sat back with a sigh once her sister had gone upstairs. It was going to be a long time before Bethany got over Jarrett. Damn him for hurting her sister! And thank God she hadn't given in to his blackmail when pressed to.

Jarrett kept to his word and came to the church on Sunday again, but he had no chance to talk to Sian this time. Chris and his parents were with her this week, and the four of them returned to the Newmans' for lunch.

Chris had remained taciturn and unapproachable, and as the wedding neared Sian could feel her own nerves stretching to breaking point, her own doubts and uncertainties beginning to take over the more withdrawn Chris became.

On the final Sunday when the banns were read her father insisted they should all go to church, and dragged the reluctant Bethany along too.

Jarrett was there again, nodding recognition as they filed into the church to sit at a pew further down from him. Sian watched Bethany closely for any reaction to the encounter, but her sister seemed as pale and composed as usual, not at all her normal self, her vivaciousness completely dulled, even her beauty subdued in her unhappiness.

As usual it was a beautiful service. The vicar was a man who talked to his congregation rather than breathing fire and brimstone on them.

Sian stiffened as he came to the banns for Chris and herself, her gaze unwillingly drawn to Jarrett. He raised dark blond eyebrows in acknowledgement and shook his head slightly.

She turned away sharply, biting her lip. He wasn't going to give up. Against all the odds—his wife, her forthcoming marriage—Jarrett still believed she would go to him.

And no matter how she denied her feelings for him she still felt aware of him whenever they were in the same room together, felt warm and loved from his gaze on her. And she couldn't see past her wedding to Chris. No matter how she tried she couldn't envisage their married life together, almost as if it were never going to happen.

Maybe it was because she wasn't actually leaving home, that she and Chris would be living with her father and Bethany. Whatever the reason, she felt a sense of unease.

And it wasn't helped by Jarrett's approach after the service, his long strides bringing him quickly to their side. His greeting was terse, his gaze narrowing on Bethany's pale face. 'How are you?' His tone was almost gentle.

Her smile was nervy, her eyes fever-bright. 'Fine—thank you,' she said huskily.

'Sian,' he nodded to her, ignoring the glowering Chris at her side. Her father was a short distance away talking to some of his friends. 'Just under a week to go to the wedding now,' he derided.

'Yes,' she acknowledged coolly.

'Is Bethany to be a bridesmaid?'

'And Chris's sister Ginny,' she said tightly, knowing his polite interest in her wedding arrangements was only skin-deep, his gaze completely calculating.

'I remember Ginny,' he nodded. 'You must be looking forward to your sister's wedding to Chris, Bethany.' His voice once again softened to gentleness.

'Don't let us keep you, King,' Chris put in abruptly. 'I'm sure a busy man like you must have somewhere else he would rather be.'

'Not particularly,' the other man drawled infuriatingly. 'I usually keep my Sundays free. Bethany, are you sure you're feeling all right?' he frowned down at her. 'You're looking very pale.'

'I—I—Excuse me!' With a choked cry Bethany ran off, and people turned to look at her as she pushed by them.

CHAPTER NINE

'BETHANY—'

'I'll go,' Chris muttered intensely.

'But—'

'Get your father to take you home,' he instructed tersely, running after Bethany.

Instead she turned furiously on Jarrett, her face white with concern 'Why couldn't you just leave her alone?' she accused heatedly.

'Me?'

'Yes—you!' she glared at him. 'You're completely selfish, Jarrett, you always were. You wanted me, so you decided to get to me any way you could, you didn't care who got hurt in the process. And that includes my young sister. You broke her heart, Jarrett—I hope you're satisfied!' She was breathing heavily in her agitation.

He grasped her arm, pulling her out of earshot of the other people gathered in the churchyard. 'I took Bethany out, on a casual basis, a couple of times,' he bit out raggedly.

'You knew she saw it as more than that!'

'I'm sure she didn't,' he shook his head. 'We had fun together, we talked. God, I think I only kissed her once or twice.'

'And we both know when that was, don't we!' Sian scorned. 'But I don't believe you, Jarrett. I know you, I know your sensuality—'

'My sex drive, you mean,' he derided hardly.

'Yes!' she hissed. 'You could never leave any woman

alone. And Bethany wouldn't be breaking her heart over a few casual dates. You warned me you would seduce her.' Sian's eyes widened accusingly. 'My God, you *did*!' she gasped.

His mouth set in a grim line. 'I didn't touch her,' he rasped. 'And if she's told you otherwise then she's lying.'

'She hasn't told me anything,' Sian said dully. 'She hasn't been talking much at all the last couple of weeks.'

'Then I suggest you look elsewhere than me for the cause of that,' he told her coldly. 'Because despite my threats to you I wouldn't harm a hair on your sister's head. How could I?' his voice lowered softly. 'When you love her.'

Sian swallowed hard, seeing the sincerity of his gaze. 'You really never meant to go through with that?'

'Never,' he said firmly.

She bit her bottom lip. 'Then I owe you an apology. I thought—I'm sorry,' she said abruptly. 'I felt sure—I have to go, Jarrett. I have to get my father. And I'm really sorry I misjudged you.'

'Sian, can we talk—'

'Not just now,' she shook her head, already looking for her father. 'I have to get home to Bethany.'

He grasped her wrist, his green eyes compelling. 'You do believe I didn't touch her?'

She couldn't doubt it. Jarrett might be many things, but he wouldn't lie to her about something as important as this. The memory of the way he had once lied to her about something just as important flashed into her mind—and was instantly dismissed.

But her shake of her head looked like denial to Jarrett. He pushed her roughly away from him. 'Go and find your father,' he instructed harshly.

'Jarrett—'

He was already walking away, and she saw her father hurrying towards her, obviously having been told of Bethany's desperate flight.

They talked little on the drive home, but they didn't see Bethany either, so Chris must have already picked her up and taken her home.

Sian knew she would have to explain to Jarrett that she had believed him, but for now that could wait. Bethany had to be her first consideration now.

Chris's car was in the driveway and she left her father parking his car on the road and went quickly into the house, the sound of murmuring voices drawing her towards the lounge. Oh, she hoped Chris had been able to calm Bethany down.

She pushed open the door, freezing in the act of speaking as she took in the scene in front of her. Bethany was crying quietly, Chris talking soothingly, his arms about her sister as he comforted her.

'Please don't cry, Bethany,' he pleaded huskily. 'It will all work out, you'll see. We'll talk to Sian, explain to her—'

'No!' Bethany cried. 'I won't have her hurt again!'

'Darling . . . !' Chris groaned before his head bent and he kissed her with demanding passion.

Sian looked at them with numbed disbelief, sure that this couldn't be happening a second time—and not with her *own sister*!

'Good God!' her father gasped behind her, having come in without Sian being aware of it, as shocked as she was by what he was witnessing.

Bethany and Chris sprang apart and turned guiltily, Bethany's expression stricken, Chris's dismayed.

To Sian it was all like a scene from a farcical comedy,

and she had played this scene before, time and time again with sickening repetition, only then it had been Jarrett with Nina Marshall; seeing Chris with Bethany just left her numb.

Her sister gave a choked cry before running out of the room, her face pale and haunted, her eyes huge troubled pools of storm-tossed blue.

'Bethany—'

'Leave her!' their father instructed Chris harshly, walking purposefully into the room. 'How dare you come here and abuse the trust you've been shown, betraying Sian's love for you?'

'George, it isn't like that,' Chris pleaded. 'I—'

'I think it would be best if you left, Chris.' The other man was watching Sian, correctly assessing the deep shock she was in. 'You and Sian have to talk, but it can't be now.'

Chris looked at Sian too, his face paling at how ill she looked. 'Darling, I'm sorry,' he moved towards her to clasp her hands, surprised at how cold they were, the day warm. 'I didn't mean for this to happen. I just didn't seem to be able to stop myself. Sian, I—'

'I said leave it, Chris,' her father spoke strongly. 'Can't you see she's almost at collapsing point?' His arms came about her protectively. 'Come back later,' he ordered the other man. 'Maybe she'll be up to listening to you then. Although I wouldn't count on it,' he added grimly as he guided Sian out of the room.

'I'll wait and talk to you now, George,' Chris told him dully. 'I'd like to explain.'

Her father nodded. 'I think someone had better start doing that,' he rasped.

Sian said nothing as her father took her upstairs to her room, although her father spoke soothingly all the time, pulling back the coverlet on the bed to help her lie down, smoothing her hair back from her brow.

'Don't think just now, Sian,' he advised softly. 'I'm sure it didn't mean anything. Bethany has been upset lately, Chris was comforting her and it got a little out of hand. I'm sure that's all it was, love.'

She looked up at him with shadowed hazel eyes. Her father hadn't heard the conversation before the kiss, or the way Chris called Bethany 'darling', but she had, and she had heard the love behind the endearment too. Whether Chris had actually said the words or not, she had a feeling he was in love with Bethany—and that she returned the feeling!

'I'll go down and talk to him now,' her father soothed. 'You just rest. You can sort this misunderstanding out with him later.'

She nodded wordlessly, knowing that her father was deeply disturbed by what was going on around him.

And she was disturbed herself, more than disturbed. Chris's taciturn moods, and Bethany's withdrawal into herself, suddenly seemed explained. Chris and Bethany were in love, with *each other*!

She turned into the pillow with a choked cry, hearing her father mutter something under his breath before he left the room.

Her father couldn't be unaware of the similarity to three years ago, the fact that Chris, like Jarrett, no longer loved her but someone else.

Her own stifled sobs were echoed from Bethany's room, and finally she couldn't stand it any longer, and got up to pull on her jacket, knowing she had to get out of the house, had to get away and think.

She could hear the two men talking together as she came down the stairs, knowing the two of them were in the lounge. Her movements out of the house were unhurried, feeling as if in a dream, a numbed haze clouding her brain so that she couldn't think any more.

But she didn't need to think to find her refuge, her walk to the willow unhurried and sure, the place where she always came to be alone, both now and in the past.

The scene of some of the most beautiful ecstasy she had ever known, the willow soon had its soothing effect on her, and with the return of feelings came the renewal of pain.

She hadn't loved Chris as she had once loved Jarrett, she knew that, had known it the moment she saw him kissing Bethany and felt betrayal rather than jealousy. But she did feel hurt at the way Chris had kept his feelings for Bethany a secret until now, a week before their own wedding should have taken place. Should have. Already she was talking in the past tense, knew there was no future for herself and Chris.

What was wrong with her that men found it so difficult to be faithful to her? What was it about her that caused men to eventually reject her?

'Sian.'

She closed her eyes at the sound of that husky voice, too vulnerable to turn and face Jarrett, knowing that if she did she would break down and tell him everything. And she didn't want his pity, followed by his triumph. She wanted—oh, she wanted—

She spun round, her eyes fever-bright, barely taking in the fact that he still wore the navy blue suit and pale blue shirt he had worn to church. His hair had grown longer since his return, long over his collar, fine lines beside his eyes and mouth adding to his maturity. Sian longed to smooth away those lines, to run her hands through the thickness of his hair, longed to touch him, to know once again the total oblivion Jarrett gave her through the senses.

'What is it?' he frowned at her wild-eyed look. 'I saw you walking this way from my hotel window,' he said slowly. 'But you didn't seem to be seeing anyone. Sian, what's happened?' His voice sharpened with concern.

'Will you make love to me?'

His frown deepened, a pulse beating erratically in his cheek. 'Sian—'

'Do you want to make love to me or don't you?' she asked shakily, her hands trembling so badly she felt as if they would never stop.

'You know I do—'

'Well?'

'Not like this, darling,' he refused softly. 'Something has happened, something that's shaken you so badly you don't know what you're doing.'

She gave a scornful laugh. 'I never knew what I was doing when you made love to me!'

His expression darkened at her bitterness. 'No,' he rasped in acknowledgement of the fact. 'Why do you want me to make love to you, Sian?' he frowned. 'Why now?'

She sighed tremulously. 'Because I need you now,' she told him softly.

He drew in a ragged breath. 'Me, Sian? Or would any man do?'

Her pride had taken a terrible beating today, her self-confidence almost nil in another man's rejection of her, and yet she knew that she wanted no one but Jarrett, that no one else would do.

'I need *you*, Jarrett,' she admitted softly.

He moved forward to take her in his arms, holding her against him, breathing in the perfume of her hair. 'Now tell me why?' he urged softly.

'Jarrett—'

'I have to know, Sian,' he looked down at her with fathomless green eyes. 'Do you love me?'

She recoiled from admitting such an emotion; she didn't want to admit to it ever again. To love meant to be hurt, betrayed, and she wouldn't let that happen to her again. Wordlessly she shook her head.

'No?' he bit out grimly.

'I can't,' she choked.

'Because of Newman!' he rasped, putting her away from him.

'Jarrett . . . !' She put out her hands to him appealingly.

'No!' he refused fiercely. 'I told you, I want you to come to me, to stay with me. I don't intend making love to you under any other circumstances.'

'Then I'd better go,' she said dully.

His eyes were narrowed. 'How is Bethany?'

'She—Fine,' she avoided.

'What was wrong with her?—she seemed very upset,' he frowned.

Again pride held her back from telling him what had happened in her home only an hour ago. 'I think it was seeing you that did it,' she said stiffly.

'Not that again,' he dismissed harshly.

She shook her head. 'I believe you didn't seduce her, Jarrett.'

'Earlier—'

'You misunderstood me,' she insisted.

'That makes a change,' he taunted. 'It's usually the other way around.'

'You've been—perfectly understandable, both now and in the past.'

'Understandable, but misunderstood,' he corrected.

'I don't think so,' she shook her head. 'In the past there was Nina, and now there's Arlette. Why do you still want *me*, Jarrett? Can't you ever be satisfied with one woman?' she choked on her pain.

'I was, and I am,' he bit out grimly. 'I've only ever wanted you.'

'And Nina?'

'Has been discussed so many times I'm tired of the subject!'

'As you tired of her,' Sian scorned. 'She's married now, you know.'

'Good for her,' he said uninterestedly.

'She came back from her trip with you to London with a brand new husband.' Sian couldn't resist trying to dent his giant ego, she was in so much pain herself she had to hit out at him somehow. She had needed him so badly just now, needed to feel wanted, and Jarrett had turned her down.

'Why not?' he shrugged. 'I'm sure that gave the gossips something else to think about.'

'I think she did it through pride as much as anything else,' Sian said hardly. 'It would have been too humiliating for her to have come back here alone after you had abandoned her.'

Jarrett's face darkened ominously. 'After I had *what*?'

'You took her to London with you, used her, and then left her behind when you went to America,' Sian accused disgustedly.

A deep coldness entered his eyes. 'I took Nina to London with me so that she could escape the scandal *you* had stirred up.'

'Me?' she gasped her outrage. 'You were the one who was having an affair with her; it was *your* scandal!'

He shook his head, his mouth tight. 'It had been over between Nina and me for months, as soon as I met you. You knew damn well it had. It was your own uncertainties, your own lack of trust that caused the scandal. I didn't want Nina, and you knew it.'

'That isn't what she said!' Sian flashed.

Jarrett's frown deepened. 'What Nina said? You actually spoke to her?'

'She spoke to me,' she recalled bitterly. 'She came to see me the day after your stag party, and she told me all about the two of you, how you'd continued to see her even though you had proposed to me.'

'Nina told you *that*?' he exploded disbelievingly.

'Yes,' she said dully.

'But it was lies,' he groaned. 'All lies! Why would she tell you something like that?' He hit the fist of one hand into the palm of the other. 'God, it's the classic tale, isn't it, a case of "a woman scorned",' he rasped. 'She lied to you, Sian. Oh yes, she did,' he insisted as she went to protest. 'She probably even set up that scene at the stag party. Oh, not that you should walk in and see us, but she probably did expect it to get back to you, might even have come and told you about it herself. We were set up, Sian, and neither of us realised it.'

'You *were* kissing her.'

'"Good luck", she said,' he murmured softly, raggedly. 'She came over to me and asked to give me a good luck kiss. No, I didn't refuse,' he said hardly. 'I was going to be your husband for the rest of our lives, I didn't think you would begrudge her one little kiss.'

Sian's head was spinning, wondering if he could possibly be telling the truth. 'You took her to London with you . . .'

'To get away from the scandal, I told you,' he said impatiently. 'Everyone was talking about us, Nina came to me and said she couldn't stand it, she had to get away for a while, and as I had already made arrangements to go to London on the Saturday she begged a ride with me. She didn't go *with* me, Sian, I just gave her a lift. We parted company as soon as we reached London.'

She moistened her suddenly dry lips, completely dazed. 'Didn't you realise the—the construction that would be put on the two of you leaving together?'

'It never occurred to me,' he shook his head. 'I wasn't thinking at all that day. I was hurting too damned much!' he admitted gruffly.

'I'm sure Nina was thinking very clearly,' Sian said softly. 'She convinced me utterly, Jarrett. She told me that your affair with her was something neither of you could help, that it would probably continue after we were married.'

'And you believed her!'

She swallowed hard, knowing she deserved his contempt. Three years, three long lonely years, when they might have been together after all.

Jarrett watched the pain flicker across her face, groaning low in his throat as he took her into his arms. 'You were a child then, Sian, you would have seen through Nina's lies if you had been older, more experienced,' he murmured into her hair. 'I wanted you as my wife then, but I think perhaps you needed this time to mature, to grow into the woman I need.'

'Are you—are you asking me to marry you?' she gasped.

'Of course,' he sounded puzzled. 'I've been asking you ever since I got back.'

'But I—What about Arlette?' She drew back to look at him.

'She's leaving for New York as soon as I can get her booked on to a plane,' he said grimly.

'And your tie to her?'

He shrugged. 'My lawyers are still working on it. If she would just agree it would make it a whole lot easier. But she's determined to hang on until the bitter end, is sure she'll get more out of me this way, more money I mean. A bulk settlement doesn't appear to be what she wants at all.'

'She wants you,' Sian told him raggedly.

'And I want you—which cancels out any other woman as far as I'm concerned.' His gaze was intent. 'Will you marry me, darling?'

Nina was in the past, and he denied there being anything between them, something she believed. But Arlette was very much in the present, a reminder that he had taken a wife after leaving her, and he had no right to propose to *her* in the circumstances.

'No!' She wrenched out of his arms, shaking her head, the tears not far from the surface. 'No, I won't marry you,' she denied strongly.

'What is it you want from me, Sian?' he demanded harshly. 'I can't help your lack of trust in the past, that's something you're going to have to live with. I've told you I love you, asked you to marry me, what more can I do?' He watched her with narrowed eyes.

'You already have a wife, how can you possibly ask me to marry you!' she choked in a pained voice. 'Or do you expect me to just live with you until you have your divorce?' she scorned brokenly.

'My—*divorce*?' he echoed softly.

'From Arlette,' she nodded impatiently.

Jarrett drew in a deep controlling breath, his mouth tight, his eyes glacial. 'Of course—Arlette,' he repeated softly. 'Who else?' He had withdrawn from her mentally as well as physically, suddenly a cold stranger. 'I think we've said all we have to say, Sian. I wish you happiness with Newman,' he added distantly.

She couldn't understand this cold withdrawal. 'Jarrett . . . ?'

He looked at her with cold contempt. 'What is it now? Some other woman I'm supposed to have lurking in my life?' he demanded bitterly. 'Well, I don't intend explaining myself to you, Sian, not any more. You've more than shown me your opinion of me. Give your love to someone like Newman,' he advised distantly. 'Someone you can *trust*.' He turned and began walking back to the town, a man with golden hair and emeralds for eyes.

Sian was crying in earnest now. Someone she could trust. How ironic that was!

CHAPTER TEN

BETHANY's wedding to Chris took place four weeks later. It was a beautiful wedding; the bride was ecstatic, the groom deliriously happy, the groom's mother less so, still confused by the change of bride.

Sian witnessed her sister's marriage to her own ex-fiancé with a sense of detachment. She had felt this way since Jarrett left for New York just over three weeks ago.

When she had got back to the house the day they had last spoken it had been to have her father gently explain that Chris and Bethany had fallen in love, that Chris had discovered his love for her sister only when Bethany had begun to see Jarrett, realising his jealousy wasn't a brotherly feeling.

'But why didn't he tell me?' she cried. 'Why leave it until now?'

'I think he thought it might only be temporary madness, that it would pass,' her father sighed.

'Bethany loves him too?'

He nodded. 'I've been up and spoken to her. She tried not to love him, Sian, tried to avoid even seeing him— that's why she's been staying in her room so much. But when she saw him at the church today she realised she loved him too,' he grimaced.

It all made sense in that moment, Chris's jealousy of Jarrett hadn't been because of her but because of Bethany, his working late and bad temper merely ways of avoiding discussing what was really bothering him.

She even had a feeling she knew the exact night Chris had told Bethany of his feelings, that Bethany's shock the evening Jarrett's wife had arrived hadn't been because of that but because Chris had just told her he loved her.

The fact that Chris and Bethany loved each other had been enough for her, and she hadn't stood in their way after that, had gone upstairs to give a very unhappy Bethany her blessing. It had taken some convincing to get Bethany to believe she really wasn't being noble, that she had felt uncertain of her own feelings for some time.

But strangely she had no longer felt uncertain; she knew that if she had to wait for Jarrett until after his divorce then she would do so. She wanted to tell him so, to tell him she loved him, wanted to be with him. A call to the Swan the next day had told her that he had already left for America, that Ida Barlowe wasn't expecting him back. And of course his wife had gone with him.

Sian kept thinking he would be back, that he had to come back, because the house was still being built. She knew, she checked on it every day, hoping that one time when she drove down there she would once again see a golden-haired, bare-chested man performing his 'labour of love' alongside his men. But Jarrett was never there, and after a month she had resigned herself to the fact that he was never coming back, that he was having the house finished to sell it. And it would sell so easily; it was a truly beautiful house, was almost finished now except for the inside décor.

'Sian,' a shy Bethany stood in front of her, ready to leave for her honeymoon with Chris. 'Sian, I want you to have this.' She held out her bouquet.

Her expression softened at the anxiety in her sister's

face, bending down to kiss her affectionately on the cheek, hugging her tightly. 'Thank you,' she said with quiet sincerity.

'Sian—'

'Be happy,' she interrupted firmly, wanting nothing to spoil Bethany's wedding day. After all the unhappiness that had gone before it the bridal couple deserved to be happy today of all days.

'We will,' Bethany promised tearfully.

'Chris is waiting,' she prompted as her sister still seemed to hesitate.

Bethany turned to give her new husband a dazzling smile. 'Not for much longer,' she murmured, looking back at Sian. 'I just wish—'

'Then don't,' she chided gently. 'On her wedding day a bride should already have everything she could ever want or need.'

Once the bride and groom had left she excused herself, the effort of appearing the doting sister proving to be a strain. Not that she didn't wish Bethany every happiness; she knew her sister and Chris were very much in love. But it became hard to act and seem happy when the man she loved was thousands of miles away, when she had lost him for ever.

She sat beside the willow looking up at the house bathed in golden sunlight, the pillars gleaming whitely, the bricks a dark red in contrast. The swimming-pool stood empty at its side with young saplings already planted at its other side. It was all as it should have been for them, and now it would belong to someone else, someone who could have no idea of the dream and love that had gone into its building.

The tears flowed unheeded down her cheeks as she thought of the life she could have had there with Jarrett, loving and being loved by him. What would it have mattered that they couldn't be married right away, that Jarrett was legally tied to another woman? What did it matter *now* that he was married to Arlette, it had been *her* he wanted, her he loved.

But not any more! her heart cried. But he had loved her for three years, could he just stop by saying he no longer did—had she? No!

She got to her feet, galvanised into action, a decision made that could, and she hoped would, change her whole life.

'What the—!' her father exclaimed as she rushed into the house a few minutes later, having come home to put his feet up now that the reception had ended, watching her as she frantically searched through the telephone book. 'Sian, what on earth is the matter?' he frowned. 'What are you doing?'

'Looking up the number for the airline,' she muttered, sighing her impatience as the right page eluded her.

'So you're going to him, are you?' her father nodded slowly.

She looked up sharply. 'Him?'

'Jarrett,' he sighed. 'You are flying to America, aren't you?'

'I—' she chewed on her bottom lip. 'I thought I might. You see, he—I—I was thinking about it,' she amended.

Her father gave an angry sigh. 'It's taken you four weeks to think about *thinking* about going to see him?' he demanded in exasperation.

'Dad!' she frowned her consternation at the rebuke in his words.

'Well, has it?'

'No, of course not,' she snapped. 'I just—It's a big

decision to make. He may just reject me.' She bit down painfully on her lip at the thought.

'Maybe he will,' her father nodded. 'But I very much doubt it. I haven't told you this before, because I didn't think it should influence your decision concerning him, but Jarrett telephoned me.'

'He did?' she gasped, momentarily diverted from looking for the telephone number she wanted. 'When?'

'A week after he left.'

'So long ago?' she groaned. 'Oh, Dad, why didn't you tell me?'

'Because he wanted to speak to me, not you! He explained all the misunderstanding about Nina Marshall, and although I found the evidence against him damning myself then I think I may be inclined to agree with him that you were too young then to take on the responsibility of a love as possessive as his was.'

'Was?' she echoed tautly.

'Is,' her father corrected dryly. 'He still loves you. I think he's the type of man who can only love once in his life. And for him you're it, for better, for worse,' he quoted the marriage ceremony. 'Sian, the man did everything but grovel at your feet, I think it's time you did some grovelling of your own. Now he obviously explained himself to me for a reason, and I think we can both guess that easily enough, can't we.'

'He wants your approval of him,' she said slowly.

'Most prospective son-in-laws do,' he derided. 'Even a man like Jarrett. Now are you going to make that call or aren't you?' His eyes were narrowed.

'I—I am,' she decided firmly.

'Good,' he nodded his approval. 'And don't worry too much about my being at the wedding,' he sighed tiredly. 'After this last month I'm off weddings. It's enough that you're leaving me to the mercy of Bethany's cooking once she gets back!'

'Oh, Dad!' she hugged him tearfully.

'Make the phone call, love,' he urged gruffly.

Flying out to New York the following day, Sian suddenly had another attack of the nerves. Jarrett might not even be *in* New York—she should have checked first! Well, if he wasn't she would find him. She had found a use for the money from selling her car after all. She would tell Jarrett how much she loved him, and if he rejected her after that she would—she would want to die! She couldn't bear to think in terms of rejection. Jarrett's call to her father hadn't been the act of a man who had fallen out of love.

But he had made no contact with *her*; she could even be married to Chris for all he seemed to care.

But none of that mattered any more, not the thought of rejection, none of it. All that really mattered now was that she should see Jarrett, at least tell him of her love for him. She had to trust in her summer madness of three years ago, had to trust in Jarrett.

New York came as a complete shock to her. Noisy and rushed, it had a charm that wasn't apparent in the television programmes that were set there. Sian felt no surprise when the cab dropped her off outside one of the high-rise buildings, King Construction Company printed in large gold letters over the long row of glass doors. She hadn't even booked into a hotel, but had come here straight from the airport. She would have plenty of time to find a hotel later if Jarrett threw her straight out! It would be no more than she deserved, she knew that.

The girls behind the reception desk gave her a curious glance, but none of them questioned her ascent in the lift to the top floor. Well, at least she hadn't been stopped at the front door!

She had never seen an office complex as luxurious as this one, and she walked through a whole office of busy secretaries before she finally came to the office of Jarrett's private secretary, a beautiful redhead in her early thirties.

Sian straightened her shoulders as the woman looked up at her enquiringly, then she walked determinedly over to the desk. 'I'd like to see Mr King, please. My name is Sian Morrissey. I'm—'

'Miss Morrissey,' the other woman gave her a friendly smile. 'I know exactly who you are.'

Sian felt as if the breath had been knocked from her body. 'You—you do?' she croaked.

'Of course,' the secretary nodded. 'I'll just tell Mr King you're here. Please take a seat,' she invited with another beaming smile.

'Er—thanks.' Sian sat down before she fell down, putting her case beside the chair.

'Mr King?' the secretary, the nameplate on her desk reading 'Carmen Ferris', spoke into the internal telephone. 'Your fiancée is here, Jarrett,' she told him warmly. 'Jarrett?' she frowned as she obviously received no answer. 'Did you hear me, I said—That's right,' she glanced over at Sian, giving her a smile of confidence. 'I'll tell her.' She rang off, and rose elegantly to her feet.

Sian watched her approach with misgivings. Was she to be rejected without even getting to see the man himself? And what on earth had prompted Carmen Ferris to announce her as his fiancée! Jarrett probably wondered what game she was playing now!

'He told me to ask if you would mind waiting?' She

gave a rueful shrug at the delay. 'He's in with his lawyer at the moment. I could get you a cup of coffee?' she offered pleasantly.

'I—That would be nice,' Sian accepted jerkily.

The woman swayed over to the pot of fresh coffee, pouring a cup for Sian and putting it on a tray with cream and sugar. 'Did you just fly over?' She eyed the single suitcase Sian had with her.

'Er—yes.' She chewed on her inner lip. 'Why did you introduce me as Jarrett's fiancée just now?'

Carmen looked surprised by the question. 'Well, you are, aren't you?' she frowned.

'I—'

The inner office door opened at that moment and a short stocky man preceded Jarrett out of the room, and the two men shook hands as Jarrett walked the lawyer to the door.

Sian took this opportunity to take in everything about him. His hair had been cut since the last time she had seen him, although it still curled attractively over the collar of his brown suit and cream shirt. His face looked leaner, harsher, his eyes hard as he turned to find her avid gaze on him. Those hard green eyes made her conscious of her own appearance, of the grey suit and black high-necked blouse she had worn for the flight over here. Could he see that she had lost weight, that her eyes were shadowed, that she had an unhappy droop to her mouth? Or did he no longer care enough to notice anything about her?

'Sian,' he bit out tersely as he walked across the room towards her, his hands on her shoulders drawing her to her feet. 'Let's go through to my office,' he suggested grimly as she quivered beneath his touch. 'Hold all my calls, Carmen,' he told the curious secretary abruptly, opening the leather-covered door for Sian to enter the inner office before him.

She had half expected the luxury that met her behind that door, the vast office that looked more like an elegant, if austere, lounge than any office she had ever seen. The only concession to an office that she could see was the huge mahogany desk in front of the window. There were also several boxes in the process of being packed with the impressive looking books from the mahogany bookcase.

'Excuse the mess,' Jarrett said curtly. 'Most of this is due to be shipped out on Friday.'

'Shipped out?' She turned to look at him, finding the door closed behind him now, so that the room was completely soundproofed. 'To England, you mean?' she frowned.

His mouth twisted. 'Of course.'

Sian moistened her lips nervously, 'You still intend going through with the move to Swannell?'

'Yes,' he nodded distantly. 'Although a smaller office will be maintained here. Sit down, won't you,' he invited tersely.

'I—I'm not sure I shall be staying' she hesitated.

Dark blond brows rose. 'You hardly came all the way to New York to leave without even saying hello,' he derided.

Sian dropped down into the waiting leather chair, sinking into its dark brown luxuriousness. She doubted she would be able to get out of it in a hurry! Although she couldn't see any reason why she would need to.

Jarrett faced her across the width of his desk, and she saw him as business opponents must see him. Formidable! His position across the desk from her also reminded her that now they were even farther apart socially; Jarrett was a successful millionaire, while she was a mere receptionist/typist. She must have been mad to come here!

His eyes narrowed to green slits. 'What are you thinking?'

'I'm thinking I made a mistake coming here. I'm sure you—'

'Never be too sure of anything about me, Sian,' he warned softly. 'Sit down!' he ordered as she tried to get to her feet, the chair proving as difficult as she had thought it would.

Her eyes widened indignantly before she lowered herself back into the chair, watching him apprehensively.

His mouth twisted. 'Surprised, aren't you?' he derided harshly. 'I think I was always too soft with you—'

'Too soft?' she repeated in an outraged voice. 'You've always bullied and bossed me around!'

'And you always knew how to reduce me to an eager lover,' he rasped. 'I should never have given in to you the first time you captured me with those huge hazel eyes of yours. I'd never let a woman call the tune in a relationship before, and I shouldn't have let you do it either.'

'But you—'

'Why are you here, Sian?' he asked impatiently. 'You surely didn't come all this way to argue with me?'

Suddenly she couldn't meet his piercing gaze; her anger died as quickly as it had flared. 'No,' she admitted huskily.

'Then why?' he bit out.

Sian swallowed hard. 'Your secretary called me your fiancée.' She couldn't answer him.

He shrugged broad shoulders beneath the expensively

tailored jacket. 'Carmen has worked for me for three years, she worked for my uncle before that,' he said as if that explained everything.

But it didn't, not to Sian. 'You mean you've never denied our engagement?' she gasped.

His mouth tightened. 'No.'

'But Arlette—'

'Yes—Arlette,' he drawled coldly, glancing at his wrist-watch. 'She should be here any moment. Your timing in arriving today is perfect, Sian. You may be able to help me celebrate the removal of Arlette from my life.'

She paled. 'I'd better leave—'

'You will stay exactly where you are,' he told her grimly. 'I haven't finished talking to you yet. Far from it!'

'But—'

'You're staying, Sian.' He stood up to come round the desk, completely menacing. 'If I have to tie you to the chair!'

At that moment the door swung open unannounced, the familiar figure of Arlette King moving gracefully into the room as the door swung shut behind her. 'Why, Miss Morrissey—how nice,' she drawled in a falsely sugary tone. 'I didn't know Miss Morrissey was to be here, Jarrett,' she looked at him questioningly.

Jarrett leant back on the side of his desk. 'Sian is full of surprises,' he mocked.

'How nice for you,' Arlette taunted.

'It can be,' he nodded.

Hard blue eyes were turned on Sian. 'How are you, Miss Morrissey—or is it Mrs Newman now?' She arched thin brows.

'No, it isn't—I mean it is.' Sian took a deep breath at

her complete lack of confidence. 'My name is still Morrissey,' she said more firmly, noticing that Jarrett didn't seem at all surprised by this disclosure.

'Then your little sister got the vet after all,' Arlette derided.

Sian's eyes widened. 'How did you know . . . ?'

The other woman shrugged. 'I saw them together one evening, talking very intensely. They made such a nice couple.'

'They're married now,' she revealed dully, knowing by the lack of change of expression in Jarrett's face that he had known that too.

'What a shame—rejected again, Sian,' Arlette scorned.

Sian stiffened. 'I prefer to think of it as realising a mistake before it was too late,' she snapped. 'Can you claim the same thing?'

'Unfortunately, no,' Arlette bit out.

'When the two of you have quite finished,' Jarrett's voice was icy. 'Can we get this over with, Arlette?'

'But of course, honey,'

'You've spoken to Gilpatrick?'

'Just now,' Arlette nodded. 'What a charming man he is.'

'Fascinating!' Jarrett derided. 'He gave you the papers?'

She nodded. 'And I signed them. He's taken them back to his office to make sure I didn't use invisible ink,' she taunted.

'I trust you,' he drawled.

'I don't think Gilpatrick does,' Arlette said dryly. 'I've cleared out my desk, Jarrett.'

'What did you take?' he snorted.

'My manicure set,' she gave a husky laugh. 'The

amount you paid me to get out I doubt I'll need to do anything but my nails for the rest of my life!'

Sian turned away, trying not to listen to what was a very personal conversation. Jarrett had no right to make her stay and listen to this. She looked up to find him watching her with puzzled eyes.

'Frank intended you to have the money and not the power, Arlette,' he said slowly. 'He intended you to sell to me for a high profit.'

'I know that,' she shrugged. 'But after he died you were still available—you can't blame me for trying to get you, using my directorship as leverage.'

'I don't blame you,' he drawled. 'But I was never available.'

Arlette sighed. 'Not to me, anyway. I did care for Frank in the beginning, Jarrett. I just—He was such a lot older than me, and—'

'You should never have married him!' Jarrett's voice was harsh.

Arlette shrugged. 'I've always liked money, and your uncle had plenty of it. He also loved me very much.'

'A fact you played upon to the full,' he snapped.

'We were happy to start with—'

'Until he became ill, then you didn't want to know!'

Arlette grimaced. 'I've never liked illness of any kind.'

'Then maybe you'd better leave, because you make me *feel* ill,' he rasped cruelly.

'Okay, I'm going,' she drawled unconcernedly. 'I doubt we'll be meeting again, so do I offer you both my congratulations?'

'No,' Jarrett rasped.

Arlette shrugged, walking over to the door. 'I'll say

goodbye, then.' The door closed behind her, but her heady perfume still filled the room.

Sian stared at the door in numbed silence. Not only had she misjudged Jarrett about Nina, but about Arlette too. Arlette had been married to Frank King, his *uncle*!

She swallowed hard. 'I—' her voice came out as a low croak. 'Oh God!' she buried her face in her hands. 'God, Jarrett, how you must hate me!' She stood blindly to her feet. 'I'll go. I should never have come here.' She walked straight into the hard wall of his chest.

'You aren't going anywhere.' Somehow his voice had gentled, his hands warm against her arms.

She collapsed weakly against his chest. 'How you must hate me,' she groaned again.

'I could never bring myself to do that,' he said gruffly. 'Tell me, Sian, if you didn't come here because you finally knew Arlette is my aunt by marriage then why did you come?'

She steadied her ragged breathing with effort, licking the tears away from her lips as she looked up at him. 'Because I love you,' she told him simply. 'Because I can't live without you any longer.'

'But if you still believed Arlette was my wife?' he frowned.

'I was willing to take what I could get,' she admitted shakily. 'To wait if you wanted to divorce her, to just live with you if you didn't. I'm still willing to do that.'

'Are you, indeed?' Jarrett drawled, putting her away from him and into a chair. 'We still have a lot of talking to do before I decide what I'm going to do with you. How did you feel when Newman married Bethany?' he scowled.

'Relieved,' she answered instantly. 'But how did you know about it?'

'I knew the engagement was off before I left Swannell,' he shrugged. 'And your father told me about the wedding.'

'If you knew I wasn't engaged—'

'Why did I leave?' he said harshly. 'I still had a lot to do here, and nothing to stay there for.'

'The house—'

'Is finished,' he nodded. 'Why did you wait until now to come to me, Sian? Did your father finally convince you about Arlette?' he asked bitterly.

'Dad?' she frowned her puzzlement. 'I doubt if he knew she was your aunt either. We all assumed—'

'Too damned much!' he rasped. 'But your father did know about Arlette, I told him when I called.'

'I didn't even know you'd called him until yesterday, after I'd told him I was coming to see you.'

'After?' he repeated softly.

'Yes. He said you'd explained about Nina, but he didn't mention Arlette. Oh, please believe me, Jarrett, I didn't know about her!' she pleaded with him.

'I could see that as I spoke to her just now—you went quite white. But why tell you about Nina and not Arlette?' he frowned.

'I think I know why,' she said quietly. 'I had to prove to you, as well as myself, that I trust you.' Her head went back. 'And I do trust you, Jarrett.'

He nodded, his mouth twisting wryly. 'Remind me to thank your father the next time I see him. When you turned up here today I thought he'd explained it all to you, that you'd decided to give me a second chance, that you'd decided to forgive and forget.' He began to pace the room. 'Only there was nothing for you to forgive, and plenty for me to forget—namely your lack of trust throughout our relationship!'

She could see he was becoming angry again, that the softness of a moment ago was fading. 'Jarrett—'

'All the time I was in Swannell this time proposing marriage to you you thought I had something a little more basic in mind—an affair!' His eyes glittered down at her. 'It seemed to me that as soon as you knew the truth about Arlette you came hotfooting it over here expecting me to welcome you with open arms. I've had too many kicks in the teeth from you in the past to do that,' he said grimly.

'But I didn't know the truth until just now,' she pleaded. 'You know I didn't.'

'When I paid off Arlette?' his mouth twisted. 'Even then you thought I was buying her out of a marriage instead of the firm.' His eyes narrowed as she blushed her guilt. 'How could you think I would ever marry a woman like Arlette?' he rasped.

'I just—She's very beautiful,' Sian said lamely.

'If you like snakes,' he dismissed harshly. 'By the time I got over here three years ago she'd curled herself about my uncle so well it was impossible to stop him marrying her, to get him to believe her affairs, to stop him leaving her the directorship in King Construction.'

'She was the reason things weren't straightforward for you? I remember you said that once.' Sian blushed at his hard look.

'I said a lot of other things you should have remembered, more important things,' he ground out. 'But you were too busy distrusting me to believe anything I had to say. Tell me, Sian, if I let you live with me what happens the next time I so much as look at a pretty woman twice?' His eyes were narrowed green slits.

She moistened her lips, refusing to think of the fact that he had said 'live with' him and not 'marry' him. She had come here to accept any terms he would give her, and that was what she would do. 'You want the truth?' Her head went back challengingly.

'Undoubtedly,' he nodded.

She shrugged. 'Then I'll probably scratch her eyes out,' she admitted simply.

Jarrett gave a shout of laughter and came over to pull her into his arms. 'I won't even look once,' he promised raggedly into her hair. 'Not when I have my fierce little tigress to come home to!'

Her arms were tight about his waist beneath his jacket, her face buried in his chest. 'You'll let me live with you?' she asked eagerly.

'Yes,' he chuckled softly, his anger completely gone now.

'Even if I am jealous and possessive?' she pointed out anxiously.

'Yes. Because I'm just as jealous and possessive,' Jarrett smiled down at her, his eyes darkening as he threaded his hands into her hair to hold her head immobile beneath him. 'God, I love you, Sian,' he groaned before his mouth captured hers.

She kissed him as if she never wanted to stop—and she didn't! She wanted him to make love to her right now, this instant.

'We can't, Sian,' he moaned against her throat as he sensed her need. 'Not here. Will you come home with me?'

'Oh yes,' she nodded eagerly.

'Sleep with me?'

'Yes.' She shivered in anticipation.

'Marry me?' Jarrett asked throatily.

Her eyes widened as she searched his face for some sign of mockery. There was none. She swallowed hard, almost afraid to believe. 'Did you say *marry* you?'

'Sian,' he said in a mocking voice, 'surely you aren't suggesting I make a dishonest woman of you?'

She touched his face gently, wonderingly. 'It's no more than I deserve. I want to marry you, I want nothing more than that,' she admitted shakily. 'But I'll understand if you want to wait, if you want to be sure before you—'

'I don't need to make sure,' he growled, his arms tight. 'I've been sure since the moment I set eyes on you three years ago.'

'Oh, Jarrett!' she hid her face in his warm throat. 'You make me feel so ashamed.'

'So you ought to be,' he admonished gently. 'But I'll spend the rest of our lives making love to you, watching you carry our children. You won't have time to be jealous again.'

Sian pouted in feigned indignation. 'I thought we were only having four children!'

'That won't stop me making love to you day and night,' he murmured against the curve of her breasts where he had unbuttoned the black blouse to his questing lips.

'Could we wait to have children?' she requested huskily. 'I don't want anything to stop my being in your arms every night for the next year or so at least.'

Jarrett laughed throatily. 'A woman after my own heart!' He was suddenly serious. 'It's all yours, Sian, it always has been. Take care of it this time, I don't function too well without it,' he admitted gruffly.

'I'll cherish it, Jarrett,' she promised softly. 'Every day of my life.'

'I know you will.' His arms tightened about her before

he reluctantly released her. 'Let's go to my flat now, I can't wait any longer for you. Tomorrow we'll see about getting married. After that we'll spend three months on a deserted island somewhere getting to know each other better.'

'*Better*?' she spluttered as they left the office hand in hand, neither of them noticing the curious looks coming their way from Jarrett's staff.

'Better,' he nodded. 'That's the way it is between us, the way it always was—it just gets better and better all the time.'

And it did seem to. That first time together in Jarrett's arms after three years, possessed by him utterly, was like a flood after a drought. And Sian looked forward to their marriage with eagerness and confidence, knowing that each of them cherished the other above life itself.

THE HISTORY OF COFFEE

"A very good drink...almost as black as ink, and very good in illness." Such is the way a sixteenth-century European physician who visited Turkey described his first drink of coffee. The Turks had learned of the pleasures of coffee from the Arabians, who probably began using it as a medicinal drink during the ninth century A.D.

By 1615 Venetian traders made it possible for Europeans to test coffee's marvelous qualities themselves, and by the 1650s the vogue for coffeehouses struck Italy, France and England.

In London, the number of coffeehouses increased rapidly — by 1715 there were 2,000 of them — and became major social and political centers. Coffee, the "drink of democracy," could be taken by any man — no women allowed! — who could pay the entrance fee of one penny, then two pennies for every cup of the liquid consumed. All classes met and mingled in packed, smoke-filled rooms, talking, trading gossip and quips, hearing and reading the news, picking up and posting mail.

Business was transacted in coffeehouses. Lloyd's, for instance, was a center for shipping and insurance. Eventually each trade, profession and political party had its preferred coffeehouse, from which modern clubs evolved.

In the early nineteenth century the coffeehouse tradition in England declined, and coffee as the great democratic brew gave way to tea. Coffee continued to be popular in continental Europe — Vienna coffeehouses are famous — and in America. People are still drawn to coffee shops and coffee breaks, anywhere or anytime they can stop to relax, read or exchange views with friends — and imbibe this stimulating brew.

Begin a long love affair with
SUPERROMANCE.
Accept LOVE BEYOND DESIRE **FREE.**

Complete and mail the coupon below today!

- -

FREE! Mail to: SUPERROMANCE

In the U.S.
2504 West Southern Avenue
Tempe, AZ 85282

In Canada
649 Ontario St.
Stratford, Ontario N5A 6W2

YES, please send me FREE and without any obligation, my
SUPERROMANCE novel, LOVE BEYOND DESIRE. If you do not hear
from me after I have examined my FREE book, please send me the
4 new **SUPERROMANCE** books every month as soon as they come
off the press. I understand that I will be billed only $2.50 for each book
(total $10.00). There are no shipping and handling or any other hidden
charges. There is no minimum number of books that I have to
purchase. In fact, I may cancel this arrangement at any time.
LOVE BEYOND DESIRE is mine to keep as a FREE gift, even if
I do not buy any additional books.

NAME _____ (Please Print)

ADDRESS _____ APT. NO. _____

CITY _____

STATE/PROV. _____ ZIP/POSTAL CODE _____

SIGNATURE (If under 18, parent or guardian must sign.)

SUP-SUB-2

This offer is limited to one order per household and not valid to present
subscribers. Prices subject to change without notice.
Offer expires August 31, 1984

134 BPS KAKM